ISAK
DINESEN
(KAREN BLIXEN)

THE DREAMING CHILD
AND OTHER STORIES

PENGUIN BOOKS

PENGUIN BOOKS

Published by the Penguin Group. Penguin Books Ltd, 27 Wrights Lane,
London w8 5TZ, England Penguin Books USA Inc., 375 Hudson Street,
New York, New York 10014, USA Penguin Books Australia Ltd, Ringwood,
Victoria, Australia. Penguin Books Canada Ltd, 10 Alcorn Avenue, Toronto,
Ontario, Canada M4V 3B2 Penguin Books (NZ) Ltd, 182-190 Wairau Road,
Auckland 10, New Zealand   Penguin Books Ltd, Registered Offices: Har-
mondsworth, Middlesex, England   **These stories have been taken from
Winter's Tales by Isak Dinesen (Karen Blixen), published by Penguin Books
in 1983.** This edition published 1995   Copyright 1942 by Random House Inc
Copyright © renewed by Johan Philip Thomas Ingerslev, 1970. All rights
reserved   Typeset by Datix International Limited, Bungay, Suffolk. Printed in
England by Clays Ltd, St Ives plc ·
10 9 8 7 6 5 4 3 2 1

CONTENTS

The Dreaming Child

In the first half of last century, there lived in Sealand, in Denmark, a family of cottagers and fishermen, who, after their native place, were called Plejelt, and who did not seem able to do well for themselves in any way. Once they had owned a little land here and there, and fishing-boats, but what they had possessed they had lost, and in their new enterprises they failed. They just managed to keep out of the jails of Denmark, but they gave themselves up freely to all such sins and weaknesses, – vagabondage, drink, gambling, illegitimate children and suicide, – as human beings can indulge in without breaking the law

The old judge of the district said of them: 'These Plejelts are not bad people, I have got many worse than they They are pretty, healthy, likeable, even talented in their way. Only they just have not got the knack of living. And if they do not promptly pull themselves together, I cannot tell what may become of them, except that the rats will eat them.'

Now it was a queer thing, – just as if the Plejelts had been overhearing this sad prophecy and had been soundly frightened by it, – in the following years, they actually seemed to pull themselves together. One of them married into a respectable peasant family, another had a stroke of luck in the herring-fishery, another was converted by the new parson of the parish, and obtained the office of bell-ringer. Only one child of the clan, a girl, did not escape its fate, but on the contrary, appeared to collect upon her young head the entire burden of guilt and misfortune of her tribe. In the course of her short, tragic life, she was washed from the country into the town of Copenhagen, and here, before she was twenty, she died in dire misery, leaving a small son behind her. The father of the child, who is otherwise unknown to this tale, had given her a hundred rixdollars; these, together with the child, the dying mother handed over to an old washerwoman, blind of one eye, and named Madam Mahler, in whose house she had lodged. She begged Madam Mahler to provide for her baby as long as the money lasted, contenting herself with a brief respite, in the true spirit of the Plejelts.

At the sight of the money, Madam Mahler got a rose in each cheek, she had never till now set eyes on a hundred rixdollars, all in a pile. As she looked at the child she sighed deeply, then she took the task upon her shoulders, with what other burdens life had already placed there.

The little boy, whose name was Jens, in this way first became conscious of the world, and of life, within the slums of old Copenhagen, in a dark back yard like a well, a labyrinth of filth, decay and foul smell. Slowly he also became conscious of himself, and of something exceptional in his worldly position. There were other children in the back yard, a big crowd of them, they were pale and dirty as himself. But they all seemed to belong to somebody, they had a father and a mother, there was for each of them a group of other ragged and squalling children whom they called brothers and sisters, and who sided with them in the brawls of the yard; they obviously made part of a unity. He began to meditate upon the world's particular attitude to himself, and upon the reason for it. Something in it responded to an apprehension within his own heart: – that he did not really belong here, but somewhere else. At night, he had chaotic, many-coloured dreams, in the daytime his thoughts still lingered in them; sometimes they made him laugh, all to himself, like the tinkling of a little bell, so that Madam Mahler, shaking her own head, held him to be a bit weak in his.

A visitor came to Madam Mahler's house, a friend of her youth, an old wry seamstress with a flat, brown face and a black wig. They called her Mamzell Ane, she had in her young days sewn in many great houses. She wore a red bow at the throat, and had many coquettish, maidenly little ways and postures with her. But within her sunk bosom she had also a greatness of soul, which enabled her to scorn her present misery in the memory of that splendour which in the past her eyes had beheld. Madam Mahler was a woman of small imagination, she did but reluctantly lend an ear to her friend's grand, indeterminate soliloquies, and after a while Mamzell Ane turned to little Jens for sympathy. Before the child's grave attentiveness, her fancy took speed, she called forth and declaimed upon the glory of satin, velvet and brocade, of lofty halls and marble staircases. The lady of the house was adorned for a ball by the light of multitudinous candles, her husband came in to fetch her with a star on his breast, while the carriage and pair waited in the street. There were big weddings in the cathedral, and funerals as well, with all the ladies swathed in black, like magnificent, tragic columns. The children called their parents Papa and Mamma, they had dolls and hobby-horses to play with, talking parrots in gilt cages, and dogs that were taught to walk on their hind legs. Their mother kissed them, gave them bonbons and pretty pet names. Even in the winter the warm rooms behind the silk curtains were filled with the perfumes of flowers named heliotropes and oleanders, and the chandeliers that hung from the ceiling were themselves made of glass, in the shape of bright flowers and leaves.

The idea of this majestic, radiant world, in the mind of little Jens merged with that of his own inexplicable isolation in life, 3 into a great dream, or fantasy. He was so lonely in Madam Mahler's house because one of the houses of Mamzell Ane's tales was his real home. In the long days when Madam Mahler stood by her wash-tub or brought her washing out into town, he fondled and played with the picture of this house and of the people who lived in it, and who loved him so dearly. Mamzell Ane, on her side, noted the effect of her *épopée* on the child, realized that she had at last found the ideal audience, and was further inspired by the discovery. The relation between the two developed into a kind of love-affair: for their happiness, for their very existence, they had become dependent upon one another.

Now Mamzell Ane was a revolutionist, – of her own accord, and out of some primitive, visionary sight within her proud, virginal heart, for she had all her time lived amongst submissive and unreflective people. The meaning and object of existence to her was grandeur, beauty and elegance. For the life of her she would not see them disappear from the earth. But she felt it to be a cruel and scandalous state of things that so many men and women must live and die without these highest human values, – yes, without the very knowledge of them, - that they must be poor, wry and inelegant. She was every day looking forward to that day of justice when the tables were to be turned, and the wronged and oppressed were to enter into their heaven of refinement and gracefulness. All the same, she now took pains not to impart into the soul of the child any of her own bitterness or rebelliousness. For as the intimacy between them grew, she did in her heart acclaim little Jens as legitimate heir to all the magnificence for which she had herself prayed in vain. He was not to fight for it, everything was his by right, and should come to him on its own. Possibly the inspired and experienced old maid also noted that the boy had in him no talent for envy or rancour whatever. In their long, happy communications, he accepted Mamzell Ane's world serenely and without misgiving, in the very manner, – except for the fact that he had not got any of it – of the happy children born within it.

There was a short period of his life in which Jens made the other children of the back yard parties to his happiness. He was, he told them, far from being the half-wit barely tolerated by old Madam Mahler, he was on the contrary, the favourite of fortune. He had a papa and mamma and a fine house of his own, with such and such things in it, a carriage, and horses in the stable. He was spoilt and would get everything he asked for. It was a curious thing that the children did not laugh at him, nor afterwards pursue him with mockery. They almost appeared to believe him. Only they could not understand or follow his fancies, they took but little interest in them, and after a while they altogether disregarded them. So Jens again gave up sharing the secret of his felicity with the world.

Still some of the questions put to him by the children had set the boy's mind working, so that he asked Mamzell Ane, – for the confidence between them by this time was complete, – how it had come to pass that he had lost contact with his home and had been taken into Madam Mahler's establishment? Mamzell Ane found it difficult to answer him, she could not explain the fact to herself. It would be, she reflected, part of the confused and corrupt state of the world in general. When she had thought the matter over, she solemnly, in the manner of a Sibyl, furnished him with an explanation. It was, she said, by no means unheard of, neither in life nor in books, that a child, particularly a child in the highest and happiest circumstances, and most dearly beloved by his parents, enigmatically vanished and was lost. She stopped short at this, for even to her dauntless and proven soul, 5 the theme seemed too tragic to be further dwelt on. Jens accepted the explanation in the spirit in which it was given, and from this moment saw himself as that melancholy, but not uncommon phenomenon: a vanished and lost child.

But when Jens was six years old, Mamzell Ane died, leaving to him her few earthly possessions: a thin-worn silver thimble, a fine pair of scissors, and a little black chair with roses painted on it. Jens set a great value to these things, and every day gravely contemplated them. Just then, Madam Mahler began to see the end of her hundred rixdollars. She had been piqued by her old friend's absorption in the child, and so decided to get her own back. From now on she would make the boy useful to her in the business of the laundry. His life therefore was no longer his own, and the thimble, the scissors and the chair stood in Madam Mahler's room, the sole tangible remnants, or proofs, of that splendour which he and Mamzell Ane had known of and shared.

At the same time as these events took place in Adelgade, there lived in a stately house in Bredgade, a young married couple, whose names were Jakob and Emilie Vandamm. The two were cousins, she being the only child of one of the big ship-owners of Copenhagen, and he, the son of that magnate's sister – so that if it had not been for her sex, the young lady would with time have become head of the firm. The old ship-owner, who was a widower, with his widowed sister occupied the two loftier lower storeys of the house. The family held closely together, and the young couple had been betrothed from childhood.

Jakob was a very big young man, with a quick head and an easy temper. He had many friends, but none of them could dispute the fact that he was growing fat at the early age of thirty. Emilie was not a regular beauty, but she had an extremely graceful and elegant figure, and the slimmest waist in Copenhagen, she was supple and soft in her walk and all her movements, with a low voice, and a reserved, gentle manner. As to her moral being, she was the true daughter of a long row of competent and honest tradesmen: upright, wise, truthful and a bit of a Pharisee. She gave much time to charitable work, and therein minutely distinguished between the deserving and the undeserving poor. She entertained largely and prettily, but kept strictly to her own milieu. Her old uncle, who had travelled round the world, and was an admirer of the fair sex, teased her over the Sunday dinner table: there was, he said, an exquisite piquancy in the contrast between the suppleness of her body, and the rigidity of her mind

There had been a time when, unknown to the world, the two had been in concord. When Emilie was eighteen, and Jakob was away in China on a ship, she fell in love with a young naval officer, whose name was Charlie Dreyer, and who, three years earlier, when he was only twenty-one, had distinguished himself and been decorated in the war of 1849. Emilie was not then officially engaged to her cousin; she did not believe, either, that she would exactly break Jakob's heart if she left him and married another man. All the same, she had strange, sudden misgivings, the strength of her own feelings alarmed her. When in solitude she pondered on the matter, she held it beneath her to be so entirely dependent on another human being. But she again forgot her fears when she was with Charlie, and she wondered and wondered that life indeed held so much sweetness.

Her best friend, Charlotte Tutein, as the two girls were undressing after a ball, said to her: 'Charlie Dreyer makes love to all the pretty girls of Copenhagen, but he does not intend to marry any of them. I think he is a Don Juan.'

Emilie smiled into the looking-glass. Her heart melted at the 7 thought that Charlie, misjudged by all the world, was known to her alone for what he was: loyal, constant and true.

Charlie's ship was leaving for the West Indies; upon the night before his departure he came out to her father's villa near Copenhagen to say goodbye, and found Emilie alone. The two young people walked in the garden; it was moonshine. Emilie broke off a white rose, moist with dew, and gave it to him. As they were parting on the road just outside the gate, he seized both her hands, drew them to his breast and in one great foaming whisper begged her, since nobody would see him walk back with her, to let him stay that night, until in the morning he must go so far away.

It is probably almost impossible to the children of a later generation to imagine or realize the horror, dread and abomination which the idea and the very word of seduction would awake in the minds of the young girls of that past age. She would not have been as deadly frightened and revolted if she found that he meant to cut her throat.

He had to repeat himself before she understood him, and as she did so the ground sank beneath her. She felt as if the one man amongst all, whom she trusted and loved, was intending to bring upon her the supreme sin, disaster and shame, was asking her to betray her mother's memory and all the maidens in the world. Her own feelings for him made her an accomplice in the crime, and she realized that she was lost: Charlie felt her wavering on her feet, and put his arms round her. In a stifled, agonized cry she tore herself out of them, fled, and with all her might pushed the heavy iron gate to, she bolted it on him as if it had been the cage of an angry lion. On which side of the gate was the lion? Her strength gave way, she hung on to the bars, while on the other side, the desperate, miserable lover pressed himself against them, fumbled between them for her hands, her clothes, and implored her to open. But she recoiled and flew, to the house, to her room, only to find there despair within her own heart and a bitter vacuity in all the world round it.

Six months later Jakob came home from China, and their engagement was celebrated amongst the rejoicings of the families. A month after she learned that Charlie had died from fever at St Thomas. Before she was twenty, she was married, and mistress of her own fine house.

Many young girls of Copenhagen married in the same way – *par dépit* – and then, to save their self-respect, denied their first love and made the excellency of their husbands their one point of honour, so that they became incapable of distinguishing between truth and untruth, lost their moral weight and flickered in life without any foothold in reality. Emilie was saved from their fate by the intervention, so to say, of the old Vandamms, her forefathers, and by the instinct and principle of sound merchantship which they had passed on into the blood of their daughter. The staunch and resolute old traders had not winked when they made out their balance-sheet, in hard times they had sternly looked bankruptcy and ruin in the face, they were the loyal, unswerving servants of facts.

So did Emilie now take stock of her profit and loss. She had loved Charlie, he had been unworthy of her love, and she was never again to love in that same way. She had stood upon the brink of an abyss, and but for the grace of God she was at this moment a fallen woman, an outcast from her father's house. The husband she had married was kind-hearted, and a good man of business, he was also fat, childish, unlike her. She had got out of life a house to her taste and a secure, harmonious position in her own family and in the world of Copenhagen; for these she was grateful, and about them she would take no risk. She did, at this moment of her life, with all the strength of her young soul, embrace a creed of fanatical truthfulness and solidity. The ancient Vandamms might have applauded her, or they might have thought her code excessive: they had taken a risk themselves, when it was needed, and they were aware that in trade it is a dangerous thing to shirk danger.

Jakob, on his side, was in love with his wife, and priced her beyond rubies. To him, as to the other young men out of the strictly moral Copenhagen bourgeoisie, his first experience of love had been extremely gross. He had preserved the freshness of his heart, and his claim to neatness and orderliness in life by holding on to an ideal of purer womanhood, in the first place represented by the young cousin, whom he was to marry, the innocent, fair-haired girl of his own mother's blood, and brought up as she had been. He carried her image with him to Hamburg and Amsterdam, and that trait in him which his wife called childishness made him deck it out like a doll or an icon, – out in China it became highly ethereal and romantic, and he used to repeat to himself little sayings of hers, to recall her low, soft voice. Now he was happy to be back in Denmark, married and in his own home, and to find his young wife as perfect as his portrait of her. At times he felt a vague longing for a bit of weakness within her, or for an occasional appeal to his own strength, which, as things were, only made him out a clumsy figure beside her delicate form. He gave her all that she wanted, and out of his pride in her superiority left her all decisions on their house and on their daily and social life. Only in their charity work, it happened that the husband and wife did not see eye to eye, and that Emilie would give him a little lecture on his credulity.

'What an absurd person you are, Jakob,' she said, 'you will believe everything that these people tell you - not because you cannot help it, but because you do really wish to believe them.'

'Do you not wish to believe them?' he asked her.

'I cannot see', she replied, 'how one can well wish to believe or not to believe. I wish to find out the truth. Once a thing is not true,' she added, 'it matters little to me whatever else it may be.'

A short time after his wedding, Jakob one day had a letter from a rejected supplicant, a former maid in his father-in-law's house, who informed him that while he was away in China, his wife had a liaison with Charlie Dreyer. He knew it to be a lie, tore up the letter, and did not give it another thought.

They had no children. This to Emilie was a grave affliction, she felt that she was lacking in her duties. When they had been married for five years Jakob, vexed by his mother's constant concern, and with the future of the firm on his mind, suggested to his wife that they should adopt a child, to carry on the house. Emilie at once, and with much energy and indignation, repudiated the idea, it had to her all the look of a comedy, and she would not see her father's firm encumbered with a sham heir. Jakob held forth to her upon the Antonines with but little effect. But when six months later he again took up the subject, to her own surprise, she found that it was no longer repellent. Unknowingly she must have given it room in her thought, and let it take root there, for by now it seemed familiar to her. She listened to her husband, looked at him, and felt kindly towards him.

'If this is what he has been looking for,' she thought, 'I must not oppose it.' But in her heart she knew, clearly and coldly, and with dread of her own coldness, the true reason for her indulgence: the deep apprehension, that when a child had been adopted there would be no more obligation on her of producing an heir to the firm, a grandson to her father, a child to her husband.

It was indeed their little divergences in regard to the deserving or undeserving poor, which brought upon the young couple of Bredgade the events recounted in this tale. In summer time, they lived within Emilie's father's villa on the Strandvej, and Jakob would drive in to town, and out, in a small gig. One day he decided to profit by his wife's absence to visit an unquestionably unworthy mendicant, an old sea-captain from one of his ships. He took the way through the ancient town, where it was difficult to get a carriage along, and where it was such an exceptional sight that people came up from the cellars to stare at it. In the narrow lane of Adelgade, a drunken man waved his arms in front of the horse, it shied, and knocked down a small boy with a heavy wheelbarrow piled high with washing, – the wheelbarrow and the washing ended sadly in the gutter. A crowd immediately collected round the spot, but expressed neither indignation nor sympathy. Jakob made his groom lift the little boy on to the seat. The child was smeared with blood and dirt, but he was not badly hurt, nor in the least scared, he seemed to take his accident as an adventure in general, or as if it had happened to somebody else.

'Why did you not get out of my way, you little idiot?' Jakob asked him.

'I wanted to look at the horse,' said the child, and added: 'Now, I can see it well from here.'

Jakob got the boy's whereabouts from an onlooker, paid him to take the wheelbarrow back, and himself drove the child home. The sordidness of Madam Mahler's house, and her own, one-eyed, blunt unfeelingness impressed him unpleasantly, still he had before now been inside the houses of the poor. But he was,

12

here, struck by a strange incongruity between the back yard and the child who lived in it. It was as if, unknowingly, Madam Mahler was housing, and knocking about a small, gentle, wild animal, or a sprite. On his way to the villa, he reflected that the child had reminded him of his wife, - he had a reserved, as it were, selfless way with him, behind which one guessed great, integrate strength and endurance.

He did not speak of the incident that evening, but he went back to Madam Mahler's house to inquire about the boy, and, after a while, he recounted the adventure to his wife and, somewhat shyly and half in jest, proposed to her that they should take the pretty, forlorn child as their own.

Half in jest, she entered into his idea; it would be better, she thought, than taking on a child whose parents she knew. After this day she herself at times opened up the matter when she could find nothing else to talk to him about. They consulted the family lawyer, and sent their old doctor to look the child over. Jakob was surprised and grateful at his wife's compliance to his wish. She listened with gentle interest when he developed his plans, and would even sometimes vent her own ideas on education.

Lately Jakob had found his domestic atmosphere almost too perfect, and had had an adventure in town, now he tired of it and finished it. He bought Emilie presents, and left her to make her own conditions as to the adoption of the child. He might, she said, bring the boy to the house on the first of October, when they had moved into town from the country, but she herself would reserve her final decision in the matter until April, when he should have been with them for six months. If by then she did not find the child fit for their plan, she would hand him over to some honest, kindly family in the employ of the firm. 13

Till April they themselves would likewise be only Uncle and Aunt Vandamm to the boy.

They did not talk to their family of the project, and this circumstance accentuated the new feeling of comradeship between them. How very different, Emilie said to herself, would the case have proved, had she been expecting a child in the orthodox mode of women. There was indeed something neat and proper about settling the affairs of nature according to your own ideas. 'And,' she whispered in her mind, as her glance ran down her looking-glass, 'in keeping your figure.'

As to Madam Mahler, when the time came to approach her, the matter was easily arranged. She had not got it in her to oppose the wishes of her social superiors, she was also, vaguely, rating her own future connection with a house that must surely turn out an abundance of washing. Only the readiness with which Jakob refunded her past outlays on the child left in her heart a lifelong regret that she had not asked for more.

At the last moment Emilie made a further stipulation. She would go alone to fetch the child. It was important that the relation between the boy and herself should be properly established from the beginning, and she did not trust to Jakob's sense of propriety upon the occasion. In this way, it came about that, when all was ready for the child's reception in the house of Bredgade, Emilie drove by herself to Adelgade to take possession of him, easy in her conscience towards the firm and her husband, but already, beforehand, a little tired of the whole affair.

In the street, by Madam Mahler's house, a number of unkempt children were obviously waiting for the arrival of the carriage, they stared at her, but turned off their eyes when she looked at them. Her heart sank as she lifted her ample silk skirt and passed through their crowd and across the back yard; would her boy have the same look? Like Jakob, she had many times before visited the houses of the poor, it was a sad sight, but it could not be otherwise: 'You have the poor with you always.' But today, since a child from this place was to enter her own house, for the first time she felt personally related to the need and misery of the world. She was seized with a new deep disgust and horror, and at the next moment with a new, deeper pity. In these two minds, she entered Madam Mahler's room.

Madam Mahler had washed little Jens and water-combed his hair. She had also, a couple of days before, hurriedly enlightened him as to the situation and his own promotion in life. But being an unimaginative woman, and moreover, of the opinion that the child was but half-witted, she had not taken much trouble about it. The child had received the information in silence, he only asked her how his father and mother had found him. 'Oh, by the smell,' said Madam Mahler.

Jens had communicated the news to the other children of the house. His papa and mamma, he told them, were coming on the morrow, in great state, to fetch him home. It gave him matter for reflection that the event should raise a great stir in that same world of the back yard that had received his visions of it with indifference. To him, the two were the same thing.

He had got up on Mamzell Ane's small chair to look out of the window and witness the arrival of his mother. He was still standing on it when Emilie came in, and Madam Mahler in vain made a gesture to chase him down. The first thing that Emilie noticed about the child was that he did not turn his gaze from hers, but looked her straight in the eyes. At the sight of her, a great, ecstatic light passed over his face. For a moment, the two looked at one another.

The child seemed to wait for her to address him, but as she 15 stood on, silent, irresolute, he spoke: 'Mamma,' he said, 'I am glad that you have found me. I have waited for you so long, so long.'

Emilie gave Madam Mahler a glance - had this scene been staged to move her heart? But the flat lack of understanding in the old woman's face excluded the possibility, and she again turned to the child.

Madam Mahler was a big, broad woman, Emilie herself, in a crinoline and a sweeping mantilla, took up a good deal of space, the child was much the smallest figure in the room, yet at this moment he dominated it, as if he had taken command of it. He stood up straight, with that same radiance in his face and countenance. 'Now I am coming home again, with you,' he said.

Emilie vaguely and amazedly realized that to the child the importance of the moment did not lie with his own good luck, but with that tremendous happiness and fulfilment which he was bestowing on her. A strange idea, that she could not have explained to herself, at that, ran through her mind, she thought: 'This child is as lonely in life as I.' Gravely she moved nearer to him and said a few kindly words.

The little boy put out his hand and gently touched the long silky ringlets that fell forward over her neck. 'I knew you at once,' he said proudly, 'you are my mamma, who spoils me. I would know you amongst all the ladies, by your long, pretty hair.' He ran his fingers softly down her shoulder and arm and fumbled over her gloved hand. 'You have got three rings on today,' he said.

'Yes,' said Emilie in her low voice.

A short, triumphant smile broke his face. 'And now you kiss me, Mamma!' he said, and then grew very pale. Emilie did not know that his excitement rose from the fact that he had never been kissed. Obediently, surprised at herself, she bent down and kissed him.

Jens's farewell to Madam Mahler at first was somewhat ceremonious for two people who had known each other a long time For she already saw him as a new person, the rich man's child, and took his hand formally, with a stiff face. But Emilie bade the boy, before he went away, to thank Madam Mahler because she had looked after him till now, and he did so with much freedom and grace. At that, the old woman's tanned and furrowed cheeks once more blushed deeply, like a young girl's, as by the sight of the money at their first meeting, - she had so rarely been thanked in her life.

In the street he stood still. 'Look at my big fat horses!' he cried.

Emilie sat in the carriage, bewildered. What was she bringing home with her from Madam Mahler's house?

In her own house, as she took the child up the stairs and from one room into another, her bewilderment grew, rarely had she felt so uncertain of herself. It was, everywhere, in the child, the same rapture of recognition - at times he would also mention and look for things which she did faintly remember from her own childhood, or other things of which she had never heard. Her small pug, that she had brought with her from her old home, yapped at the boy, she lifted it up, afraid that it would bite him.

'No, Mamma,' he cried, 'she will not bite me, she knows me well.'

A few hours ago - yes, she thought, up to the moment when in Madam Mahler's room she had kissed the child - she would have scolded him: 'Fye, you are telling a fib.' Now she said nothing, and the next moment the child looked round the room and asked her: 'Is the parrot dead?'

'No,' she answered wondering, 'she is not dead, she is in the other room.'

She realized that she was afraid both to be alone with the boy and to let any third person join them. She sent the nurse out of the room. By the time when Jakob was to arrive at the house, she listened for his steps on the stair with a kind of alarm.

'Who are you waiting for?' Jens asked her.

She was at a loss how to designate Jakob to the child. 'For my husband,' she replied, embarrassed.

Jakob on his entrance found the mother and the child gazing into the same picture book.

The little boy stared at him. 'So it is you, who is my papa!' he exclaimed. 'I thought so, too, all the time. But I could not be quite sure of it, could I? It was not by the smell that you found me, then. I think it was the horse that remembered me.'

Jakob looked at his wife, she looked into the book. He did not expect sense from a child, and was soon playing with the boy and tumbling him about.

In the midst of a game, Jens set his hands against Jakob's chest. 'You have not got your star on,' he said.

After a moment Emilie went out of the room. She thought: 'I have taken this upon me to meet my husband's wish, but it seems that I must bear the burden of it alone.'

Jens took possession of the mansion in Bredgade, and brought it to submission, neither by might nor by power, but in the quality of that fascinating and irresistible personage, perhaps the most fascinating and irresistible in the whole world: the dreamer whose dreams come true. The old house fell a little in love with him. Such is ever the lot of dreamers, when dealing with people at all susceptible to the magic of dreams. The most renowned amongst them, Rachel's son, as all the world knows, suffered hardships and was even cast in prison on that account.

Except for his size Jens had no resemblance to the classic portraits of Cupid, all the same it was evident that, unknowingly, the ship-owner and his wife had taken unto them an *amoretto*. He carried wings into the house, and was in league with the sweet and merciless powers of nature, and his relation to each individual member of the household became a kind of airy love-affair. It was upon the strength of this same magnetism, Jakob had picked out the boy as heir to the firm at their first meeting, and that Emilie was afraid to be alone with him. The old magnate and the servants of the house no more escaped their destiny – as was once the case with Potiphar, captain to the guard of Egypt; before they knew where they were, they had committed all they had into his hands.

One effect of this particular spell was this: that people were made to see themselves with the eyes of the dreamer, and were impelled to live up to an ideal, and that for this their higher existence, they became dependent upon him. During the time that Jens lived in the house, it was much changed, and dissimilar from the other houses of the town, it became a Mount Olympus, the abode of divinities.

The child took the same lordly, laughing pride in the old ship-owner, who ruled the waters of the Universe, as in Jakob's staunch, protective kindness and Emilie's silk-clad gracefulness. The old housekeeper, who had before often grumbled at her lot in life, for the while was transformed into an all-powerful, benevolent guardian of human welfare, a Ceres in cap and apron. And for the same length of time, the coachman, a monumental figure, elevated sky-high above the crowd, and combining within his own person the vigour of the two bay horses, majestically 19 trotted down Bredgade on eight shod and clattering hoofs. It was only after Jens's bed hour, when, immovable and silent, his cheek buried in the pillow, he was exploring new areas of dream, that the house resumed the aspect of a rational, solid Copenhagen mansion.

Jens was himself ignorant of his power. As his new family did not scold him or find fault with him, it never occurred to him that they were at all looking at him. He gave no preference to any particular member of the household, they were all within his scheme of things and must there fit into their place. The relation of the one to the other was the object of his keen, subtle observation. One phenomenon in his daily life never ceased to entertain and please him: that Jakob, so big, broad and fat, should be attentive and submissive to his slight wife. In the world that he had known till now, bulk was of supreme moment.

As later on, Emilie looked back upon this time, it seemed to her that the child would often provoke an opportunity for this fact to manifest itself, and would then, so to say, clap his hands in triumph and delight, as if the happy state of things had been brought about by his personal skill. But in other cases, his sense of proportion failed him. Emilie in her boudoir had an aquarium with goldfish, in front of which Jens would pass many hours, as silent as the fish themselves, and from his comments upon them, she gathered that to him they were huge, – a fine catch could one get hold of them, and even dangerous to the pug, should she happen to fall into the bowl. He asked Emilie to leave the curtains by this window undrawn at night, in order that, when people were asleep, the fish might look at the moon.

In Jakob's relation to the child there was a moment of unhappy love, or at least of the irony of fate, and it was not the first time either that he had gone through this same melancholy experience. For, ever since he himself was a small boy, he had yearned to protect those weaker than he, and to support and right all frail and delicate beings amongst his surroundings. The very qualities of fragility and helplessness inspired in him an affection and admiration which came near to idolatry.

But there was in his nature an inconsistency, such as will often be found in children of old, wealthy families, who have got all they wanted too easily, till in the end they cry out for the impossible: he loved pluck too, gallantry delighted him wherever he met it; and for the clinging and despondent type of human beings, and in particular of women, he felt a slight distaste and repugnance. He might dream of shielding and guiding his wife, but at the same time the little, cool, forbearing smile with which she would receive any such attempt from his side, to him was one of the most bewitching traits in her whole person. In this way he found himself somewhat in the sad and paradoxical position of the young lover who passionately adores virginity.

Now he learned that it was equally out of the question to patronize Jens. The child did not reject or smile at his patronage, as Emilie did, he even seemed grateful for it, but he accepted it in the part of a game or a sport. So that, when they were out walking together, and Jakob, thinking that the child must be tired, lifted him on to his shoulders, Jens would take it that the big man wanted to play at being a horse or an elephant just as much as he himself wanted to play that he were a trooper or a mahout.

Emilie sadly reflected that she was the only person in the house who did not love the child. She felt unsafe with him, even when she was unconditionally accepted as the beautiful, perfect mother, and as she recalled how, only a short time ago, she had planned to bring up the boy in her own spirit, and had written down little memorandums upon education, she saw herself as a figure of fun. To make up for her lack of feeling, she took Jens with her on her walks and drives, to the parks and the Zoo, brushed his thick hair and had him dressed up as neatly as a doll. They were always together. She was sometimes amused by his strange, graceful, dignified delight in all that she showed him, and at the next moment, as in Madam Mahler's room, she realized that however generous she would be to him, he would always be the giver. Her sisters-in-law, and her young married friends, fine ladies of Copenhagen with broods of their own, wondered at her absorption in the foundling · and then it happened, when they were off their guard, that they themselves received a dainty arrow in their satin bosoms, and between them began to discuss Emilie's pretty boy, with a tender raillery as that with which they would have discussed Cupid. They asked her to bring him to play with their own children. Emilie declined, and told herself that she must first be certain about his manners. At New Year, she thought, she would give a children's party herself.

Jens had come to the Vandamms in October, when trees were yellow and red in the parks. Then the tinge of frost in the air drove people indoors, and they began to think of Christmas. Jens seemed to know everything about the Christmas tree, the goose with roast apples, and the solemnly joyful church-going on Christmas morning. But it would happen that he mixed up these festivals with others of the season, and described how they were soon all to mask and mum, as children do at Shrovetide. It was as if, from the centre of his happy, playful world, its sundry components showed up less clearly than when seen from afar.

And as the days drew in and the snow fell in the streets of Copenhagen, a change came upon the child. He was not low in spirits, but singularly collected and compact, as if he were shifting the centre of gravitation of his being, and folding his wings. He would stand for long whiles by the window, so sunk in thought that he did not always hear when they called him, – filled with a knowledge which his surroundings could not share.

For within these first months of winter, it became evident that he was not at all a person to be permanently set at ease by what the world calls fortune. The essence of his nature was longing. The warm rooms with silk curtains, the sweets, his toys and new clothes, the kindness and concern of his papa and mamma, were all of the greatest moment because they went to prove the veracity of his visions, they were infinitely valuable as embodiments of his dreams. But within themselves they hardly meant anything to him, and they had no power to hold him. He was neither a worldling nor a struggler. He was a poet.

Emilie tried to make him tell her what he had in his mind, but got no way with him. Then one day he confided in her of his own accord.

'Do you know, Mamma,' he said, 'in my house the stair was so dark and full of holes that you had to grope your way up it, and the best thing was really to walk on one's hands and knees. There was a window broken by the wind, and below it, on the landing, there lay a drift of snow as high as me.'

'But that is not your house, Jens,' said Emilie, 'this is your house.'

The child looked round the room. 'Yes,' he said, 'this is my fine house. But I have got another house, that is quite dark and dirty. You know it, you have been there too. When the washing was hung up, one had to twine in and out across that big loft, else the huge, wet, cold sheets would catch one, just as if they were alive.'

'You are never going back to that house,' said she.

The child gave her a great, grave glance, and after a moment said: 'No.'

But he was going back. She could, by her horror and disgust of the house, keep him from talking of it, as the children there by their indifference had silenced him about his happy home. But when she found him mute and pensive by the window, or at his toys, she knew that his mind had returned to it. And now and again, when they had played together, and their intimacy seemed particularly secure, he opened on the theme.

'In the same street as my house,' he said one evening as they were sitting together on the sofa before the fireplace, 'there was an old lodging-house, where the people who had got plenty of money could sleep in beds, and the others must stand up and sleep, with a rope under their arms. One night it caught fire, and burned all down. Then, those who were in bed hardly got their trousers on, but ho! – those who stood up and slept were the lucky boys, they got out quick. There was a man who made a song about it, you know.'

There are some young trees which, when they are planted have the root twisted, and will never take hold in the soil. They may shoot out a profusion of leaves and flowers, but they must soon die. Such was the way with Jens. He had sent out his small branches upwards and to the sides, had fared excellently of the chameleon's dish and eaten air, promise-crammed, and the while he had forgotten to put out roots. Now the time came when by the law of nature, the bright, abundant bloom must needs wither, fade and waste away. It is possible, had his imagination been turned on to fresh pastures, that he might for a while have drawn nourishment through it, and have delayed his exit. Once or twice, to amuse him, Jakob had talked to him of China; the queer outlandish world captivated the mind of the child, he dwelt with the highest excitement on pictures of pigtailed Chinamen, dragons, and fishermen with pelicans, and upon the fantastic names of Hong Kong and Yangtze-kiang. But the grown-up people did not realize the significance of his novel imaginative venture, and so. for lack of sustenance, the frail, fresh branch soon drooped.

A short time after the children's party, early in the new year, the child grew pale and hung his head. The old doctor came and gave him medicine to no effect. It was a quiet, unbroken decline, the plant was going out.

As Jens was put to bed and was, so to say, legitimately releasing his hold upon the world of actuality, his fancy made headway and ran along with him, like the sails of a small boat, from which the ballast is thrown overboard. There were now, all the time, people round him, who would listen to what he said, gravely, without interrupting or contradicting him; this happy state of things enraptured him. The dreamer's sick-bed became a throne.

Emilie sat at the bed all the time, distressed by a feeling of impotence which sometimes in the night made her wring her hands. All her life she had endeavoured to sever good from bad, right from wrong, happiness from unhappiness. Here she was, she reflected with dismay, in the hands of a being, much smaller and weaker than herself, to whom these were all one, who welcomed light and darkness, pleasure and pain, in the same spirit of gallant, debonair approval and fellowship. The fact, she told herself, did away with all need of her comfort and consolation here at her child's sick-bed; it often seemed to abolish her very existence.

Now within the brotherhood of poets, Jens was a humorist, a

comic fabulist. It was, in each individual phenomenon of life, the whimsical, the burlesque moment that attracted and inspired him. To the pale, grave, young woman, his fancies seemed sacrilegious within a death-room, yet after all it was his own death-room.

'Oh, there were so many rats, Mamma,' he said, 'so many rats. They were all over the house. One came to get a bit of lard on the shelf, – pat! a rat jumped at one. They ran across my face at night. Put your face close to me, and I will show you how it felt.'

'There are no rats here, my darling,' said Emilie.

'No, none,' said he, 'when I am not sick any more, I will go back and fetch you one. The rats like the people better than the people like them. For they think us good, lovely to eat. There was an old comedian, who lived in the garret, he had played comedy when he was young, and had travelled to foreign countries. Now he gave the little girls money to kiss him, but they would not kiss him because they said that they did not like his nose. It was a curious nose, too, – all fallen in, – and when they would not, he cried, and wrung his hands. But he got ill, and died, and nobody knew about it. But when at last they went in, do you know, Mamma, – the rats had eaten off his nose – nothing else, his nose only! But people will not eat rats, even when they are very hungry. There was a fat boy named Mads in the cellar, who caught rats in many curious ways, and cooked them. But old Madam Mahler said that she despised him for it, and the children called him Rat Mads.'

Then again he would talk of her own house. 'My grandpapa,' he said, 'has got corns, the worst corns in Copenhagen. When they get very bad, he sighs and moans, he says: "There will be storms in the Chinese Sea, it is a damned business, my ships are going to the bottom." So, you know, I think that the seamen will be saying: "There is a storm in this sea, it is a damned business, our ship is going to the bottom. Now it is time that old grandpapa, in Bredgade, goes and has his corns out."'

Only within the last days of his life did he speak of Mamzell Ane. She had been, as it were, his Musa, the only person who had knowledge of the one and the other of his worlds. As he recalled her, his tone of speech changed, he held forth in a grand, solemn manner, as upon an elemental power, of necessity known to every one.

If Emilie had given his fantasies her attention, many things might have been made clear to her. But she said: 'No, I do not know her, Jens.'

'Oh, Mamma, she knows you well!' he said, 'she sewed your wedding-gown, all of white satin. It was slow work – so many fittings! And my papa,' the child went on and laughed, 'he came in to you and do you know what he said? He said: "My white rose."'

He suddenly bethought himself of the scissors which Mamzell Ane had left him, and wanted them, and this was the only occasion upon which Emilie ever saw him impatient or fretful.

She left her house, for the first time within three weeks, and went herself to Madam Mahler's house to inquire about the scissors. On the way, the powerful, enigmatical figure of Mamzell Ane took on for her the aspect of a Parca, of Atropos herself, scissors in hand, ready to cut off the thread of life. But Madam Mahler in the meantime had bartered away the scissors to a tailor of her acquaintance, and she flatly denied the existence both of them and of Mamzell Ane.

Upon the last morning of the boy's life, Emilie lifted her small pug, that had been his faithful playmate, on to the bed. Then the little dark face and the crumpled body seemed to recall to him the countenance of his friend. 'There she is!' he cried.

Emilie's mother-in-law, and the old ship-owner himself, had been daily visitors to the sick-room. The whole Vandamm family stood weeping round the bed when, in the end, like a small brook which falls into the ocean, Jens gave himself up to the boundless, final unity of dream, and was absorbed in it.

He died at the end of March, a few days before the date that Emilie had fixed to decide on his fitness for admission into the house of Vandamm. Her father suddenly determined that he must be interred in the family vault – irregularly, since he was never legally adopted into the family. So he was laid down behind a heavy wrought-iron fence, in the finest grave that any Plejelt had ever obtained.

In the following days the house in Bredgade, and its inhabitants with it, shrank and decreased. The people were a little confused, as after a fall, and seized by a sad sense of diffidence. For the first weeks after Jens's burial, life looked to them strangely insipid, a sorry affair, void of purport. The Vandamms were not used to being unhappy, and were not prepared for the sense of loss with which now the death of the child left them. To Jakob, it seemed as if he had let down a friend, who had after all, laughingly trusted in his strength – now nobody had any use for it, and he saw himself as a freak, the stuffed puppet of a colossus. But with all this, after a while there was also in the survivors, as ever at the passing away of an idealist, a vague feeling of relief.

Emilie alone of the house of Vandamms, preserved, as it were, her size, and her sense of proportion. It may even be said that when the house tumbled from its site in the clouds, she upheld and steadied it. She had deemed it affected in her to go into mourning for a child that was not hers, and while she gave up the balls and parties of the Copenhagen season, she went about her domestic tasks quietly as before. Her father and her mother-in-law, sad and at a loss in their daily life, turned to her for balance, and because she was the youngest amongst them, and seemed to them in some ways like the child that was gone, they transferred to her the tenderness and concern which had formerly been the boy's, and of which they now wished that they had given him even more. She was pale from her long watches at the sick-bed, so they consulted between them, and with her husband, on means of cheering and distracting her.

But after some time Jakob was struck with her silence and scared by it. It seemed at first as if, except for her household orders, she found it unnecessary to speak, and later on as if she had forgotten or lost the faculty of speech. His timid attempts to inspirit her so much appeared to surprise and puzzle her, that he lacked the spirit to go on with them.

A couple of months after Jens's death, Jakob took his wife for a drive by the road which runs from Copenhagen to Elsinore, along the Sound. It was a lovely, warm and fresh day in May. As they came to Charlottenlund he proposed to her that they should walk through the wood, and send the carriage round to meet them. So they got down by the forest gate, and for a moment with their eyes followed the carriage, as it rolled away on the road.

They came into the wood, into a green world. The beech-trees had been out for three weeks, the first mysterious translucence of early May was over. But the foliage was still so young that the green of the forest world was the brighter in the shade. Later on, after midsummer, the wood would be almost black in the shade, and brilliantly green in the sun; now, where the rays of the sun fell through the tree crowns, the ground was colourless, dim, as if powdered with sun-dust. But where the wood lay in shadow, it glowed and luminesced like green glass and jewels. The anemones were faded and gone, the young fine grass was already tall. And within the heart of the forest, the woodruff was in bloom · its layer of diminutive, starry, white flowers seemed to float round the knotty roots of the old grey beeches, like the surface of a milky lake, a foot above the ground. It had rained in the night; upon the narrow road the deep tracks of the wood-cutter's cart were moist. Here and there, by the roadside, a grey, misty globe of a withered dandelion caught the sun; the flower of the field had come on a visit to the wood.

They walked on slowly. As they came a little way into the wood, they suddenly heard the cuckoo, quite close. They stood still and listened, then walked on. Emilie let go her husband's arm to pick up from the road the shell of a small, pale-blue bird's egg, broken in two, she tried to set it together, and kept it on the palm of her hand. Jakob began to talk to her of a journey to Germany that he had planned for them, and of the places that they were to see. She listened docilely, and was silent.

They had come to the end of the wood. From the gate they had a great view over the open landscape. After the green sombreness of the forest, the outside world seemed unbelievably light, as if bleached by the luminous dimness of midday. But after a while the colours of fields, meadows and dispersed groups of trees defined themselves to the eye, one by one. There was a faint blue in the sky, and faint, white, cumulus clouds rose along the horizon. The young green rye in the fields was about to ear; where the finger of the breeze touched it, it ran in long, gentle billows along the ground. The small, thatched peasants' houses lay like lime-white, square isles within the undulating land; round them the lilac hedges bore up their light foliage and, at the top, clusters of pale flowers. They heard the rolling of a carriage on the road in the distance, and above their heads the incessant singing of innumerable larks.

By the edge of the forest, there lay a wind-felled tree. Emilie said: 'Let us sit down here a little.'

She loosened the ribbons of her bonnet and laid it in her lap. After a minute, she said: 'There is something I want to tell you,' and made a long pause.

All through this conversation in the wood she behaved in the same way, with a long silence before each phrase – not exactly as if she were collecting her thoughts, but as if she was finding speech in itself laborious or deficient.

She said: 'The boy was my own child.'

'What are you talking about?' Jakob asked her.

'Jens,' she said, 'he was my child. Do you remember telling me that when you saw him the first time, you thought he was like me? He was indeed like me; he was my son.'

Now Jakob might have been frightened, and have believed her to be out of her mind. But lately, to him, things had come about in unexpected ways, he was prepared for the paradoxical. So he sat quietly on the trunk, and looked down on the young beech-shoots in the ground.

'My dear,' he said, 'my dear, you do not know what you say.'

She was silent for a while, as if distressed by his interruption of her train of thought. 'It is difficult for other people to understand, I know;' she said at last, patiently, 'if Jens had been here still, he might perhaps have made you understand, better than I. But try,' she went on, 'to understand me. I have thought that you ought to know. And if I cannot speak to you, I cannot speak to anyone.' She said this with a kind of grave concern, as if really threatened by total incapacity of speech.

He remembered how, during these last weeks, he had felt her silence heavy on him, and had tried to make her speak of something, – of anything.

'No, my dear,' he said, 'you speak, I shall not interrupt you.'

Gently, as if thankful for his promise, she began: 'He was my child, and Charlie Dreyer's. You met Charlie once in papa's house. But it was while you were in China that he became my lover.'

At these words, Jakob remembered the anonymous letter he had once received. As he recalled his own indignant scouting of the slander and the care with which he had kept it from her, it seemed to him a curious thing that after five years, he was to have it repeated by her own lips.

'When he asked me,' said Emilie, 'I stood for a moment in great danger. For I had never talked with a man of these matters. Only with Aunt Malvina and with my old governess. And women, for some reason, I do not know why, will have it that such a demand is a base and selfish thing in a man, and an insult to a woman. Why do you allow us to think that of you? You, who are a man, will know that he asked me out of his love and out of his great heart, from magnanimity. He had more life in him than he himself needed. He meant to give that to me. It was life itself, yes, it was eternity that he offered me.

'And I, who had been taught so wrong, I might easily have rejected him. Even now, when I think of it, I am afraid, as of death. Still I need not be so, for I know for certain that if I were back at that moment again, I should behave in the same way as I did then. And I was saved out of the danger. I did not send him away. I let him walk back with me, through the garden – for we were down by the garden gate – and stay with me that night till, in the morning, he was to go so far away.'

She again made a long pause, and went on: 'All the same, because of the doubt and the fear of other people that I had in my heart, I and the child had to go through much. If I had been a poor girl, with only a hundred rixdollars in all the world, it would have been better, for then we should have remained together. Yes, we went through much.

'When I found Jens again, and he came home with me,' she took up her narrative after a silence, 'I did not love him. You all loved him, only I myself did not. It was Charlie that I loved. Still I was more with Jens than any of you, he told me many things, which none of you heard. I saw that we could not find another such as he, that there was none so wise.' She did not know that she was quoting the Scripture, any more than the old ship-owner had been aware of doing so when he ordained Jens to be buried in the field of his fathers and the cave that was therein – this was a small trick peculiar to the magic of the dead child.

'I learned much from him. He was always truthful, like Charlie. He was so truthful that he made me ashamed of myself. Sometimes I thought it wrong in me to teach him to call you Papa.

'At the time when he was ill,' she said, 'what I thought of was this: that if he died I might, at last, go into mourning for Charlie.' She lifted up her bonnet, gazed at it and again dropped it. 'And then, after all,' she said, 'I could not do it.' She made a pause. 'Still, if I had told Jens about it, it would have pleased him, it would have made him laugh. He would have told me to buy grand, black clothes, and long veils.'

It was a lucky thing, Jakob reflected, that he had promised her not to interrupt her tale. For had she wanted him to speak he would not have found a word to say. As now she came to this point in her story she sat in silence for a long time, so that for a

33

moment he believed that she had finished, and at that a choking sensation came upon him, as if all words must needs stick in his throat.

'I thought,' she suddenly began again, 'that I would have had to suffer, terribly even, for all this. But no, it has not been so. There is a grace in the world, such as none of us have known about. The world is not a hard or severe place, as people tell us. It is not even just. You are forgiven everything. The fine things of the world you cannot wrong or harm, they are much too strong for that. You could not wrong or harm Jens, no one could.

'And, now, after he has died,' she said, 'I understand everything.'

Again she sat immovable, gently poised upon the tree stem. For the first time during their talk she looked around her, her gaze ran slowly, almost caressingly, along the forest scenery.

'It is difficult,' she said, 'to explain what it feels like to understand things. I have never been good at finding words, I am not like Jens. But it has seemed to me ever since March, since the spring began, that I have known well why things happened, why, – for instance, – they all flowered. And why the birds came. The generosity of the world, papa's and your kindness too! As we walked in the wood today, I thought that now I have got back my sight, and my sense of smell, from when I was a little girl. All things here tell me, of their own, what they signify.' She stopped, her gaze steadying. 'They signify Charlie,' she said. After a long pause she added: 'And I, I am Emilie. Nothing can alter that either.'

She made a gesture as if to pull on her gloves that lay in her bonnet, but she put them back again, and remained quiet, as before.

'Now I have told you all,' she said. 'Now you must decide what we are to do.

'Papa will never know,' she said gently and thoughtfully. 'None of them will ever know Only you. I have thought, if you will let me do so, that you and I, when we talk of Jens,' - she made a slight pause, and Jakob thought: 'She has never talked of him till today' - 'might talk of all these things too.

'Only in one thing,' she said slowly, 'am I wiser than you. I know that it would be better, much better, and easier for both you and me, if you would believe me.'

Jakob was accustomed to take a quick summary of a situation, and to make his dispositions accordingly. He waited a moment, after she had ceased to talk, to do so now.

'Yes, my dear,' he said, 'that is true.'

The Sailor-boy's Tale

The barque *Charlotte* was on her way from Marseilles to Athens, in grey weather, on a high sea, after three days' heavy gale. A small sailor-boy, named Simon, stood on the wet, swinging deck, held on to a shroud, and looked up towards the drifting clouds, and to the upper topgallant yard of the mainmast.

A bird, that had sought refuge upon the mast, had got her feet entangled in some loose tackle-yarn of the halliard, and, high up there, struggled to get free. The boy on the deck could see her wings flapping and her head turning from side to side.

Through his own experience of life, he had come to the conviction that in this world everyone must look after himself, and expect no help from others. But the mute, deadly fight kept him fascinated for more than an hour. He wondered what kind of bird it would be. These last days a number of birds had come to settle in the barque's rigging: swallows, quails, and a pair of peregrine falcons; he believed that this bird was a peregrine falcon. He remembered how, many years ago, in his own country and near his home, he had once seen a peregrine falcon quite close, sitting on a stone and flying straight up from it. Perhaps this was the same bird. He thought: 'That bird is like me. Then she was there, and now she is here.'

At that a fellow feeling rose in him, a sense of common tragedy; he stood looking at the bird with his heart in his mouth. There were none of the sailors about to make fun of him; he began to think out how he might go up by the shrouds to help the falcon out. He brushed his hair back and pulled up his sleeves, gave the deck round him a great glance, and climbed up. He had to stop a couple of times in the swaying rigging.

It was indeed, he found when he got to the top of the mast, a peregrine falcon; as his head was on a level with hers, she gave up her struggle, and looked at him with a pair of angry, desperate yellow eyes. He had to take hold of her with one hand while he got his knife out and cut off the tackle-yarn. He was scared as he looked down, but at the same time he felt that he had been ordered up by nobody, but that this was his own venture, and this gave him a proud, steadying sensation, as if the sea and the sky, the ship, the bird and himself were all one. Just as he had freed the falcon, she hacked him in the thumb, so that the blood ran, and he nearly let her go. He grew angry with her, and gave her a clout on the head, then he put her inside his jacket, and climbed down again.

When he reached the deck, the mate and the cook were standing there, looking up; they roared to him to ask what he had had to do on the mast. He was so tired that the tears were in his eyes; he took the falcon out and showed her to them, and she kept still within his hands. They laughed and walked off. Simon set the falcon down, stood back and watched her; after a while he reflected that she might not be able to get up from the slippery deck, so he caught her once more, walked away with her and placed her upon a bolt of canvas. A little after, she began to trim her feathers, made two or three sharp jerks forward, and then suddenly flew off. The boy could follow her flight above the troughs of the grey sea; he thought: 'There flies my falcon.'

When the *Charlotte* came home, Simon signed on board another ship, and two years later he was a light hand on the schooner *Hebe* lying at Bodo, high up on the coast of Norway, to buy herrings.

To the great herring markets of Bodo, ships came together from all corners of the world; here were Swedish, Finnish and Russian boats, a forest of masts, and on shore a turbulent, irregular display of life, with many languages spoken, and mighty fights. On the shore, booths had been set up, and the Lapps, small yellow people, noiseless in their movements, with watchful eyes, whom Simon had never seen before, came down to sell bead-embroidered leather-goods. It was April, the sky and the sea were so clear that it was difficult to get the eyes up against them, – salt, infinitely wide, and filled with bird shrieks, as if someone were incessantly whetting invisible knives on all sides, high up in Heaven.

Simon was amazed at the lightness of these April evenings. He knew no geography, and did not assign it to the latitude, but he took it as a sign of an unwonted goodwill in the Universe, a favour. Simon had been small for his age all his life, but this last winter he had grown, and had become strong of limb. That good luck, he felt, must spring from the very same source as the sweetness of the weather, from a new benevolence in the world. He had been in need of such encouragement, for he was timid by nature; now he asked for no more. The rest he felt to be his own affair. He went about slowly and proudly.

One evening he was ashore with land-leave, and walked up to the booth of a small Russian trader, a Jew who sold gold watches. All the sailors knew that his watches were made from bad metal, and would not go, still they bought them, and paraded them about. Simon looked at these watches for a long time, but did not buy. The old Jew had divers goods in his shop, and amongst others a case of oranges. Simon had tasted oranges on his journeys; he bought one and took it with him. He meant to go up on a hill, from where he could see the sea, and suck it there.

As he walked on, and had got to the outskirts of the place, he saw a little girl in a blue frock, standing at the other side of a fence and looking at him. She was thirteen or fourteen years old, as slim as an eel, but with a round, clear, freckled face, and a pair of long plaits. The two looked at one another.

'Who are you looking out for?' Simon asked, to say something. The girl's face broke into an ecstatic, presumptuous smile.

'For the man I am going to marry, of course,' she said.

Something in her countenance made the boy confident and happy, he grinned a little at her. 'That will perhaps be me,' he said.

'Ha, ha,' said the girl, 'he is a few years older than you, I can tell you.'

'Why,' said Simon, 'you are not grown up yourself.'

The little girl shook her head solemnly. 'Nay,' she said, 'but when I grow up I will be exceedingly beautiful, and wear brown shoes with heels, and a hat.'

'Will you have an orange?' asked Simon, who could give her none of the things she had named.

She looked at the orange and at him.

'They are very good to eat,' said he.

'Why do you not eat it yourself, then?' she asked.

'I have eaten so many already,' said he, 'when I was in Athens. Here I had to pay a mark for it.'

'What is your name?' asked she.

'My name is Simon,' said he, 'what is yours?'

'Nora,' said the girl, 'what do you want for your orange now, Simon?'

When he heard his name in her mouth, Simon grew bold. 'Will you give me a kiss for the orange?' he asked.

Nora looked at him gravely for a moment. 'Yes,' she said, 'I should not mind giving you a kiss.'

He grew as warm as if he had been running quickly; when she stretched out her hand for the orange he took hold of it. At that moment somebody in the house called out for her.

'That is my father,' said she, and tried to give him back the orange, but he would not take it. 'Then come again tomorrow,' she said quickly, 'then I will give you a kiss.' At that she slipped off; he stood and looked after her, and a little later went back to his ship.

Simon was not in the habit of making plans for the future, and now he did not know whether he would be going back to her or not.

The following evening he had to stay on board, as the other sailors were going on shore, and he did not mind that either. He meant to sit on the deck with the ship's dog, Balthasar, and to practise upon a concertina that he had purchased some time ago. The pale evening was all round him, the sky was faintly roseate, the sea was quite calm, like milk and water, only in the wake of the boats going inshore it broke into streaks of vivid indigo. Simon sat and played; after a while his own music began to speak to him so strongly that he stopped, got up and looked upwards. Then he saw that the full moon was sitting high on the sky.

The sky was so light that she hardly seemed needed there, it was as if she had turned up by a caprice of her own, she was round, demure and presumptuous. At that he knew that he must go ashore whatever it was to cost him. But he did not know how to get away since the others had taken the yawl with them. He stood on the deck for a long time, a small lonely figure of a sailor-boy on a boat, when he caught sight of a yawl coming in from a ship farther out, and hailed her. He found that it was the Russian crew from a boat named *Anna*, going ashore. When he could make himself understood to them, they took him with them; they first asked him for money for his fare, then, laughing, gave it back to him. He thought: 'These people will be believing that I am going into town, wenching,' - and then he felt, with some pride, that they were right, although at the same time they were infinitely wrong, and knew nothing about anything.

When they came ashore, they invited him to come in and drink in their company, and he would not refuse because they had helped him. One of the Russians was a giant, as big as a bear, he told Simon that his name was Ivan. He got drunk at once, and then fell upon the boy with a bear-like affection, pawed him, smiled and laughed into his face, made him a present of a gold watch-chain, and kissed him on both cheeks. At that, Simon reflected that he also ought to give Nora a present when they met again, and as soon as he could get away from the Russians, he walked up to a booth that he knew of, and bought a small blue silk handkerchief, the same colour as her eyes.

It was Saturday evening, and there were many people amongst the houses, they came in long rows, some of them singing, all keen to have some fun in the night. Simon, in the midst of this rich, bawling life under the clear moon, felt his head light with the flight from the ship and the strong drinks; he crammed the handkerchief in his pocket, it was silk, which he had never touched before, a present for his girl.

He could not remember the path up to Nora's house, lost his way, and came back to where he had started. Then he grew deadly afraid that he should be too late, and began to run. In a small passage between two wooden huts, he ran straight into a big man, and found that it was Ivan once more. The Russian folded his arms round him and held him. 'Good. Good,' he cried in high glee, 'I have found you, my little chicken. I have looked for you everywhere, and poor Ivan has wept because he lost his friend.'

'Let me go, Ivan,' cried Simon.

'Oho,' said Ivan, 'I shall go with you and get you what you want. My heart and my money are all yours, all yours, I have been seventeen years old myself, a little lamb of God, and I want to be so again tonight.'

'Let me go,' cried Simon, 'I am in a hurry.'

Ivan held him so that it hurt, and patted him with his other hand. 'I feel it, I feel it,' he said, 'now trust to me, my little friend. Nothing shall part you and me. I hear the others coming, we will have such a night together as you will remember when you are an old grandpapa.'

Suddenly he crushed the boy to him, like a bear that carries off a sheep. The odious sensation of male bodily warmth, and the bulk of a man close to him, made the lean boy mad. He thought of Nora waiting, like a slender ship in the dim air, and of himself, here, in the hot embrace of a hairy animal. He struck Ivan with all his might.

'I shall kill you, Ivan,' he cried out, 'if you do not let me go.'

'Oh, you will be thankful to me later on,' said Ivan and began to sing.

Simon fumbled in his pocket for his knife, and got it opened. He could not lift his hand, but he drove the knife, furiously, in under the big man's arm. Almost immediately he felt the blood spouting out, and running down in his sleeve.

Ivan stopped short in the song, let go his hold of the boy and gave two long, deep grunts; the next second he tumbled down on his knees. 'Poor Ivan, poor Ivan,' he groaned. He fell straight on his face.

At that moment Simon heard the other sailors coming along, 42 singing, in the by-street.

He stood still for a minute, wiped his knife, and watched the blood spread into a dark pool underneath the big body; then he ran. As he stopped for a second to choose his way, he heard the sailors behind him scream out, over their dead comrade. He thought: 'I must get down to the sea, where I can wash my hands.' But at the same time, he ran the other way. After a little while, he found himself on the path that he had walked on the day before, and it seemed as familiar to him, as if he had walked it many hundred times in his life.

He slackened his pace to look round, and suddenly saw Nora standing on the other side of the fence; she was quite close to him when he caught sight of her in the moonlight. Wavering and out of breath, he sank down on his knees; for a moment he could not speak.

The little girl looked down at him. 'Good evening, Simon,' she said in her small coy voice, 'I have waited for you a long time,' and after a moment she added: 'I have eaten your orange.'

'Oh, Nora,' cried the boy. 'I have killed a man.'

She stared at him, but did not move. 'Why did you kill a man?' she asked after a moment.

'To get here,' said Simon, 'because he tried to stop me. But he was my friend.' Slowly he got on to his feet. 'He loved me!' the boy cried out, and at that burst into tears.

'Yes,' said she slowly and thoughtfully. 'Yes, because you must be here in time.'

'Can you hide me?' he asked, 'for they are after me '

'Nay,' said Nora, 'I cannot hide you. For my father is the parson here at Bodo, and he would be sure to hand you over to them, if he knew that you had killed a man.'

'Then,' said Simon, 'give me something to wipe my hands on.'

'What is the matter with your hands?' she asked and took a little step forward.

He stretched out his hands to her.

'Is that your own blood?' she asked.

'No,' said he, 'it is his.'

She took the step back again.

'Do you hate me now?' he asked.

'No, I do not hate you,' said she. 'But do put your hands behind your back.'

As he did so she came up close to him, at the other side of the fence, and clasped her arms round his neck. She pressed her young face to his, and kissed him tenderly. He felt her face, cool as the moonlight, upon his own, and when she released him, his head swam, and he did not know if the kiss had lasted a second or an hour.

Nora stood up straight, her eyes wide open. 'Now,' she said slowly and proudly. 'I promise you that I will never marry anybody, as long as I live.'

The boy kept standing with his hands at his back, as if she had tied them there.

'And now,' she said, 'you must run, for they are coming.'

They looked at one another. 'Do not forget Nora,' said she.

He turned and ran.

He leapt over a fence, and when he was down amongst the houses, he walked. He did not know at all where to go. As he came to a house, from where music and noise streamed out, he slowly went through the door. The room was full of people, they were dancing in there. A lamp hung from the ceiling, and shone down on them, the air was thick and brown with the dust rising from the floor. There were some women in the room, but many

of the men danced with each other, and gravely or laughingly stamped the floor. A moment after Simon had come in, the crowd withdrew to the walls to clear the floor for two sailors, who were showing a dance from their own country.

Simon thought: 'Now, very soon, the men from the boat will come round to look for their comrade's murderer, and from my hands they will know that I have done it.'

These five minutes during which he stood by the wall of the dancing-room, in the midst of the gay, sweating dancers, were of great significance to the boy. He, himself, felt it, as if during this time he grew up, and became like other people. He did not entreat his destiny, nor complain. Here he was, he had killed a man, and had kissed a girl, he did not demand any more from life, nor did life now demand more from him. He was Simon, a man like the men round him, and going to die, as all men are going to die.

He only became aware of what was going on outside him, when he saw that a woman had come in, and was standing in the midst of the cleared floor, looking round her. She was a short, broad, old woman, in the clothes of the Lapps, and she took her stand with such majesty and fierceness as if she owned the whole place. It was obvious that most of the people knew her, and were a little afraid of her, although a few laughed: the din of the dancing-room stopped when she spoke.

'Where is my son?' she asked in a high shrill voice, like a bird's.

The next moment her eyes fell on Simon himself, and she steered through the crowd, which opened up before her, stretched out her old skinny, dark hand, and took him by the elbow. 'Come home with me now,' she said, 'you need not dance here tonight. You may be dancing a high enough dance soon.'

Simon drew back, for he thought that she was drunk. But as

she looked him straight in the face with her yellow eyes, it seemed to him that he had met her before, and that he might do well in listening to her.

The old woman pulled him with her across the floor, and he followed her without a word.

'Do not birch your boy too badly, Sunniva,' one of the men in the room cried to her. 'He has done no harm, he only wanted to look at the dance.'

At the same moment, as they came out through the door, there was an alarm in the street, a flock of people came running down it, and one of them, as he turned into the house, knocked against Simon, looked at him and the old woman, and ran on.

While the two walked along the street, the old woman lifted up her skirt, and put the hem of it into the boy's hand. 'Wipe your hand on my skirt,' she said. They had not gone far before they came to a small wooden house, and stopped, the door to it was so low that they must bend to get through it. As the Lapp woman went in before Simon, still holding on to his arm, the boy looked up for a moment. The night had grown misty, there was a wide ring round the moon.

The old woman's room was narrow and dark, with but one small window to it, a lantern stood on the floor and lighted it up dimly. It was all filled with reindeer-skins and wolf-skins, and with reindeer horn, such as the Lapps use to make their carved buttons and knife-handles, and the air in here was rank and stifling.

As soon as they were in, the woman turned to Simon, took hold of his head, and with her crooked fingers parted his hair and combed it down in Lapp fashion; she clapped a Lapp cap on him and stood back to glance at him. 'Sit down on my stool, now,' she said. 'But first take out your knife.'

She was so commanding in voice and manner that the boy could not choose but to do as she told him; he sat down on the stool, and he could not take his eyes off her face, which was flat and brown, and as if smeared with dirt in its net of fine wrinkles. As he sat there, he heard many people come along outside, and stop by the house, then someone knocked at the door, waited a moment and knocked again.

The old woman stood and listened, as still as a mouse.

'No,' said the boy and got up. 'This is no good, for it is me that they are after. It will be better for you to let me go out to them.'

'Give me your knife,' said she. When he handed it to her, she stuck it straight into her thumb, so that the blood spouted out, and she let it drop all over her skirt. 'Come in, then,' she cried.

The door opened, and two of the Russian sailors came and stood in the opening, there were more people outside. 'Has anybody come in here?' they asked. 'We are after a man who has killed our mate, but he has run away from us. Have you seen or heard anybody this way?'

The old Lapp woman turned upon them, and her eyes shone like gold in the lamplight. 'Have I seen or heard anyone?' she cried, 'I have heard you shriek murder all over the town. You frightened me, and my poor silly boy there, so that I cut my thumb as I was ripping the skin rug that I sew, the boy is too scared to help me, and the rug is all ruined. I shall make you pay me for that. If you are looking for a murderer, come in and search my house for me, and I shall know you when we meet again.'

She was so furious that she danced where she stood, and jerked her head like an angry bird of prey.

The Russian came in, looked round the room, and at her and

her blood-stained hand and skirt. 'Do not put a curse on us now, Sunniva,' he said timidly. 'We know that you can do many things when you like. Here is a mark to pay you for the blood you have spilled.'

She stretched out her hand, and he placed a piece of money in it.

She spat on it. 'Then go, and there shall be no bad blood between us,' said Sunniva, and shut the door after them. She stuck her thumb in her mouth, and chuckled a little.

The boy got up from his stool, stood straight up before her and stared into her face, he felt as if he was swaying high up in the air, with but a small hold.

'Why have you helped me?' he asked her.

'Do you not know?' she answered. 'Have you not recognized me yet? But you will remember the peregrine falcon that was caught in the tackle-yarn of your boat, the *Charlotte*, as she sailed in the Mediterranean? That day you climbed up by the shrouds of the topgallant mast to help her out, in a stiff wind, and with a high sea. That falcon was I. We Lapps often fly in such a manner, to see the world. When I first met you I was on my way to Africa, to see my younger sister and her children; she is a falcon too, when she chooses. By that time, she was living at Takaunga, within an old ruined tower, which down there they call a minaret.'

She swathed a corner of her skirt round her thumb, and bit at it. 'We do not forget,' she said, 'I hacked your thumb, when you took hold of me, it is only fair that I should cut my thumb for you tonight.'

She came close to him, and gently rubbed her two brown, claw-like fingers against his forehead. 'So you are a boy,' she said, 'who will kill a man rather than be late to meet your sweetheart? We hold together, the females of this earth. I shall mark your forehead now, so that the girls will know of that, when they look at you, and they will like you for it.' She played with the boy's hair, and twisted it round her finger.

'Listen, now, my little bird,' said she, 'my great grandson's brother-in-law is lying with his boat by the landing-place at this moment, he is to take a consignment of skins out to a Danish boat. He will bring you back to your boat, in time, before your mate comes. The *Hebe* is sailing tomorrow morning, is it not so? But when you are on board, give him back my cap for me.'

She took up his knife, wiped it in her skirt and handed it to him. 'Here is your knife,' she said. 'You will stick it into no more men, you will not need to, for from now you will sail the seas like a faithful seaman. We have enough trouble with our sons as it is.'

The bewildered boy began to stammer his thanks to her.

'Wait,' said she, 'I shall make you a cup of coffee, to bring back your wits, while I wash your jacket.'

She went and rattled an old copper kettle upon the fireplace; after a while she handed him a bit of strong black drink in a cup without a handle to it. 'You have drunk with Sunniva now,' she said. 'You have drunk down a little wisdom, so that in the future all your thoughts shall not fall like raindrops into the salt sea.'

When he had finished and set down the cup, she led him to the door and opened it to him. He was surprised to see that it was almost clear morning. The house was so high up that the boy could see the sea from it, and a milky mist above it. He gave her his hand to say goodbye.

She stared into his face. 'We do not forget,' she said. 'And you, you knocked me on the head there, high up on the mast. I shall give you that blow back.' With that she smacked him on the ear as hard as she could, so that his head swam.

49

'Now we are quit,' she said, gave him a great, mischievous, shining glance, and a little push down the doorstep, and nodded to him.

In this way, the sailor-boy got back to his ship, which was to sail the next morning, and lived to tell the story.

Peter and Rosa

One year, a century ago, spring was late in Denmark. In the last days of March the Sound was ice-bound, and blind, from the Danish to the Swedish coast. The snow in the fields and on the roads thawed a little in the day to freeze again at night; the earth and the air were equally without hope or mercy.

Then one night, after a week of raw and clammy fog, it began to rain. The hard, inexorable sky over the dead landscape broke, dissolved into streaming life, and became one with the ground. On all sides the incessant whisper of falling water re-echoed, it increased and grew into a song. The world stirred beneath it, things drew breath in the dark. Once more it was announced to the hills and valleys, to the woods and to the chained brooks: 'You are to live.'

In the parson's house at Søllerød his sister's son, fifteen-year-old Peter Købke, sat by a tallow candle over his *Fathers of the Church*, when through the rustle of the rain his ear caught a new sound, and he left the book, got up and opened the window. How the noise of the rain rose then! But he listened to other, magic voices within the night. They came from above, out of the ether itself, and Peter lifted his face to them. The night was dark, yet this was no longer winter gloom, it was pregnant with clarity, and as he questioned it, it answered him. And over his head called the music of wandering life in the skies. Wings sang up there, clear flutes played, shrill pipe-signals were exchanged high up beyond his head. It was the trekking birds on their way up north.

He stood for a long time thinking of them; he let them pass before the eyes of his mind one by one. Here travelled long wedges of wild geese, flights of fen-duck and teal, with the shelduck, for which one lies in wait in the late, warm evenings of August. All the pleasures of summer drew their course across the sky, a migration of hope and joy journeyed tonight, a mighty promise, set out to many voices.

Peter was a great huntsman, and his old gun was his dearest possession, his soul ascended to the sky to meet the soul of the wild birds. He knew well what was in their hearts. Now they cried: 'Northward! Northward!' - They pierced the Danish rain with their stretched necks, and felt it in their small clear eyes. They hastened away to the northern summer of play and change, where the sun and the rain share the infinite vault of heaven between them, they went off to the innumerable, nameless, clear lakes and to the white summer nights of the north. They hurried forth to fight and to make love. Higher up, in the lofts of the world, perhaps big swarms of quails, thrushes and snipes were on the move. Such a tremendous stream of longing, on its way to its goal, passed above his head, that Peter, down on the ground, felt his limbs ache. He flew a long way with the geese.

Peter wanted to go to sea, but the parson held him to his books. Tonight, in the open window, he slowly and solemnly thought his past and his future over, and vowed to run away and become a sailor. At this moment he forgave his books, and no longer planned to burn them all up. Let them collect dust, he thought, or fall into the hands of dusty people, fit for books He himself would live under sails, on a swinging deck, and would watch a new horizon rise with each morning's sun. As he had taken this resolution he was filled with such deep gratitude that he folded his hands upon the window-sill. He had been piously brought up, his thanks were dedicated to God, but they wandered a little on their way, as if beaten off their course by the rain; he thanked the spring, the birds and the rain itself.

Within the parson's house, death was zealously kept in view and lectured upon, and Peter, in his survey of the future, also took the sailor's end into consideration. His mind dwelt for some time on his last couch, at the bottom of the sea. Soberly, his brows knitted, he contemplated, as it were, his own bones upon the sand. The deep-water currents would pass through his eyes, like a row of clear, green dreams, – big fish, whales even, would float above him like clouds, and a shoal of small fishes might suddenly rush along, an endless streak, like the birds tonight. It would be peaceful, he reflected, and better than a funeral at Søllerød, with his uncle in the pulpit.

The birds travelled forth over the sound, through the strips of grey rain. The lights of Elsinore glimmered deep below, like a fragment of the Milky Way. A salt wind met them as they came out beyond the open water of the Kattegat. Long stretches of sea and earth, of woods, waste land and moors, swept south under them in the course of the night.

At dawn they sank through the silvery air, and descended upon a long file of flat and bare holmes. The rocks shone roseate as the sun came up, little glints of light came trickling upon the wavelets. The rays of the morning refracted within the ducks' own fine necks and wings. They cackled and quacked, picked and preened their feathers, and went to sleep, with their heads under their wings.

A few days later, in the afternoon, the parson's daughter Rosa stood by her loom, on which she had just set up a piece of red-and-blue cotton. She did not work at it, but looked out through the window. Her mind was balancing upon a thin ridge, from which at any moment it might tumble either into ecstasy at the new feeling of spring in the air, and at her own fresh beauty, – or, on the other side, into bitter wrath against all the world.

Rosa was the youngest of three sisters, the two others had both married and gone away, one to Møen and one to Holstein. She was a spoilt child in the house, and could say and do what she liked, but she was not exactly happy. She was lonely, and in her heart she believed that, some time, something horrible would happen to her.

Rosa was tall for her age, with a round face, a clear skin and a mouth like Cupid's bow. Her hair curled and crisped so obstinately that it was difficult to her to plait it, and her long eyelashes gave her the air of glancing at people from an ambush. She had on an old, faded blue winter frock, too short in the sleeves, and a pair of coarse, patched shoes. But the ease and gracefulness of her body lent to the rough clothes a classical and pathetic majesty.

Rosa's mother had died at her birth, and the parson's mind was fixed upon the grave. Even the daily life of the parsonage was run with a view to the world hereafter; the idea of mortality filled the rooms. To grow up in the house was to the young people a problem and a struggle, as if fatal influences were dragging them the other way, into the earth, and admonishing them to give up the vain and dangerous task of living. In her own way Rosa meditated upon death as much as Peter. But she disliked the thought of it, she was not even allured by the picture of Paradise with her mother in it, and she trusted that she would live a hundred years still.

All the same during this last winter she had often been so weary of, so angry with, her surroundings that in order to escape and punish them she had wished to die. But as the weather changed she too had changed her mind. It was better, she thought, that the others should all die. Free from them, and alone, she would walk over a green earth, pick violets and watch the plovers flitting low over the fields; she would make pebbles leap on the water, and bathe undisturbed in the rivers and the sea. The vision of this happy world had been so vivid with her that she was surprised when she heard her father scolding Peter in the next room, and realized that they were both still with her.

This spring Rosa had a particular grudge against fate. She felt it strongly, yet she did not like to admit it to herself.

Peter, her orphan cousin, had been adopted into the house nine years ago, when both he and Rosa were six years old. She could still, if she wanted to, recall the time when he had not been there, and remember the dolls, who, with the arrival of the boy, had faded out of her existence. The two children got on well, for Peter was a good-natured creature and easy to dominate, and they had then had many great adventures together

But two years ago Rosa grew up taller than the boy And at the same time she came into possession of a world of her own, inaccessible to the others, as the world of music is inaccessible to the tone-deaf. Nobody could tell where her world lay, neither did the substance of it lend itself to words. The others would never understand her, were she to tell them that it was both infinite and secluded, playful and very grave, safe and dangerous. She could not explain, either, how she herself was one with it, so that through the loveliness and power of her dream-world she was now, in her old frock and botched shoes, very likely the loveliest, mightiest and most dangerous person on earth. Sometimes, she felt, she was expressing the nature of the dream-world in her movements and her voice, but she was then speaking a language of which they had no knowledge. Within this mystic garden of hers she was altogether out of the reach of a clumsy boy with dirty hands and scratched knees; she almost forgot her old playfellow.

Then last winter Peter had suddenly, as it were, caught her up. He became the taller of the two by half a head, and this time, Rosa reflected with bitterness, he would remain so. He became so much stronger than she that it alarmed and offended the girl. On his own he began to play the flute. Peter was of a philosophical turn of mind, and, seven or eight years ago, when the two were walking together, he had often held forth to Rosa on the elements and order of the Universe, and on the curious fact that the moon, when quite young and tender, was let out to play at the hour when the other children were put to bed, but that when she grew old and decrepit she should be chased out early in the morning, when other old people like to stay in bed. But he had never talked much in the presence of his elders, and when Rosa ceased to take an interest in his enterprises or reflections, he had withdrawn into himself. Now lately he would, uninvitedly, and before the whole household, give vent to his own fancies about the world, and many of them rang strangely in Rosa's mind, like echoes of hers. At such moments she fixed her gaze hard on him, seized by a deep fear. She could no longer, she felt, be sure of her dream-world. Peter might find the 'Sesame' which opened it, and encroach upon it, and she might meet him there any day.

It was to her as if she had been betrayed by this boy, whom she had treated kindly when he was a child. His figure began to bar her outlook and to deprive her of air within her own house, to which he had really no right. From the talk of the grown-up people Rosa had guessed Peter to be an illegitimate child. This fact, if he had been a girl, would have filled her with compassion, she would have seen her playmate in the light of romance and tragedy. Now, as a boy, he came in for his part of the perfidy of that unknown seducer, his father. During the months of the long winter she had sometimes found herself wishing that he might go to sea, and there meet with a sudden death before, through him, worse things should happen to her. Peter was a wild, foolhardy boy, so she was free to hope.

Of all these strong emotions within the girl's bosom Peter knew nothing at all. In his own way he had loved Rosa from the time when he first came into the parson's house, amongst the people there she was the only one in whom he had confidence. He had suffered by her capriciousness, and yet he somehow liked it well, as he liked everything about her. Of late he was sometimes disappointed when he found it impossible to rouse her sympathy in such things as mattered to him; he then even deemed her a little shallow and silly. But on the whole, human beings, their nature and their behaviour to him, played but a small part in Peter's sphere of thought, and ranged there only just above books. The weather, birds and ships, fish and the stars, were to him phenomena of far greater moment. On a shelf in his room he kept a barque that he had carved and rigged with much precision and patience; it meant more to him than the goodwill or displeasure of anybody in the house. From the beginning, it is true, the barque had been named *Rosa*, but it would be difficult to decide whether this was meant to be a compliment to the ship or to the girl.

The girl Rosa did not weave, but looked out through the window. The garden was still winterly bare and bleak, but there was a faint silvery light in the sky, water dripped from the roof and from the boughs of every tree, and the black earth showed in the garden paths where the snow had melted away. Rosa 57 beheld it all, as grave and wistful as a Sibyl, but in reality she thought about nothing.

The parson's wife, Eline, came into the room holding her small son by the hand. The parson's wife had been his house-keeper till he married her, four years ago, and the gossips of the parish thought that she had been more. She was only half her husband's age, but she had worked hard all her life and looked older than her years. She had a brown, bony, patient face and was light of foot and movement, with a soft voice. Her life with the parson was often burdensome to her, for he had soon repented of his infidelity to the memory of his first wife, who was his own cousin, a dean's daughter and a virgin when he married her In his heart he did not recognize the peasant-woman's son either, as equal to his daughters. But Eline was a simple creature, anchored in the resigned philosophy of the peasants; she aspired to no higher position in the house than that which she had held there from the beginning. She left her husband in peace when he did not call her, and was a handmaid to her pretty stepdaughter.

Rosa in all divergences in the household sided with the wife. She was fond of her little brother, and had installed him in the parsonage as the one person beside herself entitled to have his own ways in everything,   in the manner of a monarch who acclaims another: 'Brother. Your Majesty.' But the child did not lend itself to be spoilt. In this house, overhung by the shadow of the grave, the other young people strove to keep alive, only the youngest inhabitant, the small, pretty child, seemed to fall in quietly with its doom, to withhold himself from life and to welcome extinction, as if he had only reluctantly consented to come into the world at all.

The parson's wife sat down demurely on the edge of a chair,

and let her industrious hands rest in her lap, upon her blue apron.

'No, your father will not buy the cow,' she said and sighed a little. 'They would sell that brindled cow at Christiansminde for thirty rixdollars. She is a fine cow, to calve in six weeks. But your father was angry with me when I asked him for it. For how do I know, he says, but that the day of judgment and the return of Christ may be nearer than anybody suspects? We should not hoard up treasures in this world, he says. Still,' she added and sighed again, 'we could do with the cow over the summer, in any case.'

Rosa frowned, but she could not collect her thoughts sufficiently to be really angry with her father. 'He will have to buy her in the end,' she said coldly.

A butterfly that kept alive through the winter and had woken up with the first rays of spring, was fluttering towards the light, beating its wings on the window-pane as in a succession of little, gentle finger-taps. The child had kept his eyes on it for some time, now, in a great, steady glance he imparted his discovery to Rosa.

'My brother', said Eline, 'went to have a look at the cow. She is a good cow, and gentle. I could milk her myself.'

'Yes, that is a butterfly,' said Rosa to the child. 'It is pretty. I will catch it for you.'

As she tried to take hold of it the butterfly suddenly flew up to the top of the window. Rosa pushed off her shoes and climbed on to the window-sill. But up there, above the world, she realized that the prisoner wanted to get out, and to fly. She remembered the white butterflies of last summer, flitting over the lavender borders in the garden, her heart became light and great, and she felt sorry for the captive.

'Look, we will let her out,' she said to the boy. 'Then she will fly away.'

She pushed the window open and wafted off the butterfly. The air outside was as fresh as a bath, she drew it in deeply.

At that moment Peter came up the garden path from the stable. At the sight of Rosa in the window he stood dead still.

Since on the night of the rain he had resolved to run away to sea his heart had been filled with ships: schooners, barques, frigates. Now Rosa in her stockinged feet, with the skirt of her blue frock caught back by the crossbar of the window, was so like the figurehead of a big, fine ship that for an instant he saw, so to say, his own soul face to face. Life and death, the adventures of the seafarer, destiny herself, here stood straight up in a girl's form.

It dawned upon him that long ago, when he was a child, something similar had happened to him, and that the world then held much sweetness. It is often the adolescent, the being just out of childhood, who most deeply and sadly feels the loss of that simple and mystic world. He did not speak, he was uncertain of how to address a figure-head, but as he stared at her she looked back at him, candidly and kindly, her thoughts with the butterfly. It seemed to him then that she was promising him something, a great happiness, and within a sudden, mighty motion he decided to confide in her, and to tell her all.

Rosa stepped down from the window and into her shoes, at ease with the world. She had made a butterfly happy, she had made a child happy and a boy, – were it only the silly boy Peter, – all in a movement, and with a glance. They knew now that she was good, a benefactress to all living creatures. She wished that she could have stayed up there. But as this could not be, and as she saw Peter remaining immovable in the same place before her window, she went out and stood in the garden door.

The boy flushed as he saw her so close to him. He came up to her and took hold of her wrist, beneath the scanty sleeve.

'Rosa,' he said, 'I have a great secret which nobody in the world must know. I will tell it to you.'

'What is it?' asked Rosa.

'No, I cannot tell it here,' said he, 'others might overhear us. All my life depends upon it.'

They looked at one another gravely.

'I shall come up to you tonight,' said Peter, 'when they are all asleep.'

'No, they will hear you, then,' said she, for her room was upstairs, in the gable of the house, and Peter's below

'No. Listen,' he said, 'I shall set the garden ladder up to your window. Leave it open for me. I shall get in that way.'

'I do not know if I will do that,' said Rosa.

'Oh do not be a fool, Rosa,' cried the boy. 'Let me come in. You are the only one in the world whom I can trust.'

When they were children, and had been planning some great enterprise, Peter sometimes came to Rosa's room at night. She bethought herself of it, and for a moment there was in her heart, as in his, a longing for the lost world of childhood.

'Maybe I will do it,' she said, as she freed her arm of his grip.

The night was misty, but this was the first night after the equinox in which one felt the sweet lengthening of daylight. Peter sat still till he had seen the lamp put out in the parson's room, then he went out. He rocked the ladder to the gable wall, raised it to Rosa's window, and scratched his hand in the effort. When he tried the window it was unfastened, and his heart began to beat. He swung himself into the room, and slowly and noiselessly crossed the floor. In the dark he ran his hand over the bed to make sure that the girl was in it, for she neither stirred nor said a word. Then he sat down on the bed, and for a while he was as silent as she.

The prospect of opening his mind to a friend who would not interrupt him or laugh at him, rendered him as pensive and grateful as when he had listened to the trekking birds. He remembered that it was a long time, years perhaps, since he had talked like this to Rosa. He did not know whether the fault had lain with her or with him, in either case it seemed a sad thing. Now, he reflected, it would be difficult to him to express himself. When in the end he spoke the words came tardily, one by one.

'Rosa,' he said, 'you must try to understand me, even if I speak badly.' He drew in his breath deeply.

'I have been wrong all my life, Rosa,' he said, 'but it has not been made clear to me till now.

'You know that there are people in the world called atheists, terrible blasphemers, who deny the existence of God? But I have been worse than they. I have injured God and have done him harm. I have annihilated God.'

He spoke in a low, stifled voice, with long pauses between the phrases, hampered by his own strong emotion, and by his fear of waking up the people in the house.

'For you see, Rosa,' he said, 'a man is no more than the things he makes, – whether he builds ships, or makes clocks or guns, – or even books, I dare say. You cannot call a man fine, or great, unless what he makes be great. It is so with God as well, Rosa. If the work of God does not glorify him, how can God be glorious? – And I, I am the work of God.

'I have looked at the stars,' he went on, 'at the sea and the trees, and at the beasts and birds, too. I have seen how well they come in with the ideas of God, and become what He means them to be. The sight of them must be satisfactory and encouraging to God. Just as when a boatmaker builds a boat, and she turns out a smart, seaworthy boat. I have thought, then, that the sight of me will make God sad.'

As he paused to collect his thoughts he heard Rosa draw her breath gently. He was thankful to her because she did not speak.

'I saw a fox the other day,' he took up his theme, after a long silence, 'by the brook in the birch-wood. He looked at me, and moved his tail a little. I reflected, as I looked back at him, that he does excellently well at being a fox, such as God meant him to be. All that he makes or thinks is just fox-like, there is nothing in him, from his ears to his brush, which God did not wish to be there, and he will not interfere with the plan of God. If a fox were not so, a beautiful and perfect thing, God would not be beautiful and perfect either.

'But here am I, Peter Købke,' he said. 'God has made me, and may have taken some trouble about it, and I ought to do him honour, as the fox does. But I have crossed his plans instead. I have worked against him, just because the people by me, such people as are called your neighbours, have wished me to do so. I have sat in a room for years and years and have read books, because your old father wishes me to become a clergyman. If God had wished me to be a clergyman, surely he would have made me like one, – it would even have been a small matter to him, who is almighty. He can do it when he wants, you know, he has made many clergymen. But me, he has not made me that way, I am a slow learner, you know yourself that I am dull. I have become so stale and hard that I feel it in my own bones, an ugly thing to have in the world, with reading these *Fathers of the Church*. And in that way I have made God stale and ugly as well.

'Why must we try to please our neighbour?' he went on

thoughtfully, after a pause. 'He does not know what is great, he cannot invent the fine things of the world any more than we can ourselves. If the fox had asked people what they wanted him to be, if he had even asked the King, a poor thing he would have become. If the sea had asked people what they wanted her to be they would have made but a muddle of her, I tell you. And what good can one do to one's neighbour, after all, even if one tries? It is God whom we must serve and please, Rosa. Yes, even if we could only make God glad for a moment, that would be a great thing.

'If I speak badly,' he said after a silence, 'you must believe me all the same. For I have thought about these things for a very long time, and I know that I am right. If I am no good, God is no good.'

Rosa agreed with most of what he said. To her the surest proof of the magnificence of Providence was the fact that she was there, Rosa, by the grace of God lovely and perfect. As to his view of her neighbour she was not certain. She held, that she might do a great deal to her neighbour. Neither do men light a candle, – Rosa, – and put it under a bushel, but on a candlestick, and she giveth light unto all that are in the house. Still if Peter could speak in this way he was a companion in the house, and might, surprisingly, be of use to her some time. She smiled a little on her pillow.

'And yet,' said Peter in such a great outburst of passion that against his own will his voice rose and broke. 'I love God beyond everything. I think of the glory of God before anything else.'

He became afraid that he had spoken too loud, and kept perfectly still for a few minutes.

'Move in a little, can you,' he said to the girl, 'so that I can lie there too. There is room enough for both of us.'

Without a sound Rosa withdrew to the wall, and Peter lay down beside her. The boy never washed more than was strictly needed, and smelt from earth and sweat, but his breath was fresh and sweet in the dark, close to her face.

With the horizontal position calm came to him, and he spoke less wildly. 'And all this,' he said very slowly, 'has come about only because I have not run away.'

'Run away?' said Rosa, speaking for the first time.

'Yes,' said he. 'Yes, listen, I shall run away to sea, to be a sailor. God means me to be a sailor, that is what he has made me for. I shall become a great sailor, as good as any he has ever made. To think of it, Rosa! that God made those great seas, and the storms in them, the moon shining on them, - and that I have left them alone and have never gone to see them! I have sat in that room downstairs and stared at things six inches off my nose. God must have disliked looking my way.

'Nay, imagine now, Rosa,' he said after a while, 'imagine only, - just in order to understand what I say, - that a flutemaker made a flute, and that nobody ever played on it. Would not that be a shame and a great pity? Then, all at once, someone takes hold of it and plays upon it, and the flutemaker hears, and says: "That is my flute."' He once more drew in his breath deeply, and there was a long silence in the bed.

'But', said Rosa in a small, clear voice, 'I have often wished that you would go to sea.'

At this unexpected and amazing expression of sympathy Peter became perfectly still. He had a friend in the world, then, an ally. For a long time he had failed to value his friend rightly, he had even held her to be light-headed and frivolous. And the while she had been faithful, she had thought of him, and had guessed his needs and his hopes. In this calm and fresh hour of the spring night the sweetness of true human intercourse was, for the first time, mysteriously, revealed to him.

In the end he timidly asked the girl: 'How did you come to think of that?'

'I do not know,' said Rosa, and really at this moment she had forgotten why she had wanted Peter to go to sea.

'Will you help me to run away, then?' he asked, lowly and giddily.

'Yes,' said she, and after a while: 'How am I to help you?'

'Listen,' he said, and eagerly moved a little closer to her. 'It is at Elsinore that you will get your ship. I know of a ship, the *Esperance*, the captain Svend Bagge, that lies at Elsinore now. She would take me. But I cannot get to Elsinore, your father would not let me go. Only you might tell him that you want to go to see your godmother there, and that you do not care to travel alone, and then he might let me come with you.

'And when we are there, Rosa, when we are at Elsinore I shall get on board the *Esperance* before anybody can know of it. I shall be on the North Sea before they have got the scent of it, and nearing Dover, England, Rosa. Some day I shall round the Horn.' He had to stop, he had too much to tell her, now that at last he had got himself under sail. 'But I can stay here all night,' he thought, 'I can easily stay here till morning.'

Rosa did not answer at once, it was as well that he should be kept in suspense a little, and learn to appreciate her help. 'You have thought it all out very precisely,' she said at last, with a bit of irony.

He thought her words over. 'No,' he said. 'No, I did not exactly think it out. It all came to me on its own, suddenly, and do you know when? When I saw you standing in the window.'

He was shy of telling her that she had looked like the figurehead of the *Esperance* itself, but there was so much joyful triumph in his whisper that Rosa understood without words.

After a minute she said, 'Many ships go down, Peter. Most sailors are drowned in the end.'

He had to fetch his mind back from the picture of her in the window, before he could speak. 'Yes, I know,' he said. 'But all people are to die some time, you know. And I think that to be drowned will be the grandest death of all.'

'Why do you think that?' asked Rosa, who was herself scared of water.

'Oh I do not know,' said he, and after a moment: 'It will be, perhaps, because of that great lot of water. For when you come to think of it, there is really nothing dividing the one ocean from the other. They are all one. When you drown in the sea, it is all the seas of the world that take you. It seems to me that that is grand.'

'Yes, it may be,' said Rosa.

Peter, in talking of the oceans, had made a great gesture and had struck Rosa's head. He felt her soft, crispy hair towards his palm, and beneath it her little hard, round skull. Once more he became very still. Against his own will his fingers fumbled over her head, and played with and stroked her hair. He drew his hand back, and after a minute he said: 'Now I must go.'

'Yes,' said she.

He got out of the bed and stood beside it in the dark. 'Good night,' he said.

'Good night,' said the girl.

'Sleep well,' said Peter, who had never in his life wished anybody to sleep well.

'Sleep well, Peter,' said Rosa.

Peter came down the ladder in such a state of rapture and bliss that he might as well have gone the other way, heavenwards, to those well-known stars which were now hidden behind the mist. The causes of his agitation were, on the one hand, his flight and his future at sea, and on the other: Rosa. Under ordinary circumstances the two ecstasies would have seemed to be incompatible. But tonight all elements and forces of his being were swept together into an unsurpassed harmony. The sea had become a female deity, and Rosa herself as powerful, foamy, salt and universal as the sea. For a moment he thought of reclimbing the ladder. His soul, indeed, went up, and once more embraced Rosa in the transport of glorious fellowship. His body would have followed it if he had not, bewilderedly, realized that he did not know what to do with it, once he got it there. So he sat down on the lowest round of the ladder, his head in his hands, in mystic concord with all the world.

After a time his thoughts began to adjust themselves. There was after all, a distinction between his attitude towards the Universe round him and that towards the girl above him.

In regard to the world, mankind in general and his own fate, he was from now on the challenger, and the conqueror. They would have to give themselves up to him, if they did strike he would strike back, and he would take from them what he wanted. On their side everything was clear as daylight, bright like metal, or like the surface of the sea, shining with danger, venture, victory.

But towards Rosa all his being went forth in a tremendous motion of munificence and magnanimity, in the desire to give. He had no earthly riches with which to reward her, and even if he had possessed all the treasures of the world he would have forgotten them now. It was something more absolute which he meant to yield up to her, it was himself, the essence of his nature, and at the same time it was eternity. The offering, he felt, would be the highest triumph and the utmost sacrifice of which he were capable. He could not go away until it had been consummated.

Would Rosa understand him then, would she receive him, and accept his gift? As slowly his mind swung from marine adventures and exploits to the girl, he saw that on her side everything lay in a solemn and sacred darkness, such as will be found, he thought, in the deep waters of the oceans, off sounding. It seemed that he did not know her, as she knew him. His thoughts, even, could not get quite close to her, but were held back, every time, as by an unknown law of gravitation. His wild, overwhelming longing to beatify her, and this new, strange unapproachableness of her figure to his imagination, kept him awake, in his own bed, till morning. He remembered Jacob, who had wrestled all night with the angel of God. Only here he somehow appropriated to himself the part of the angel, and reversed the cry of the Patriarch's heart. His soul called out to Rosa: 'Thou shalt not let me go except I bless thee.'

In her room upstairs Rosa, a little while after Peter had left her, turned on her side, her cheek upon her folded hands and her long plait in her bosom, as she used to do in the evening, when she meant to fall asleep. But she felt, wonderingly, that tonight she would not sleep at all. She had read about people passing a sleepless night, but as a rule they were either miscreants or rejected lovers, and it was, she reflected, a curious thing that one might be sleepless with content and ease as well. She kept on thinking of the hour that Peter had passed in her bed. A faint scent of his hair lingered on the pillow. She would not for all the world have moved any closer to the place where he had lain, but remained squeezed up against the wall, as she had been while he was there.

All, she repeated in her thoughts, had come to him on its own, suddenly, when he saw her standing in the window. She vaguely remembered that she had, not long ago, distrusted her old playmate, and had meant to refuse him access to her own secret world. Some of the things which Peter had said tonight might quite well have been said there. 'You are a silly girl, Rosa,' she whispered, as when she had been scolding her dolls.

The idea of his strength, that had alarmed her, was now pleasing to her mind. She recalled an incident of which she had not thought for many years. A short time after Peter had first come to the house he and she had had a great fight. She had pulled his hair with all her might while, with his tough boy's arms round her, he had tried to fling her to the floor. At the memory she laughed, with her eyes closed. Peter, when he climbed down the ladder, had failed to shut the window quite behind him, the night air was cold in the room. Half an hour after Peter had gone Rosa fell into a sweet, quiet sleep.

But towards morning she had a terrible dream, and woke up with her face bathed in tears. She sat up in bed, her hair sticking to her wet cheeks. She could not recollect the dream in full, she only knew that within it she had been let down and deserted by someone, and left in a cold world, from which all colour and life were gone. She tried to chase off the dream by turning to the world of realities, and to her daily life. But as she did so she remembered Peter, and the fact that he was running away to sea. At that she grew very pale.

Yes, he was running away, that was his thanks to her for letting him come into her bed, and for liking him, since last night, better than other people. She went through their night's talk, sentence by sentence. She had meant to be sweet to him, – before she went to sleep had she not, in her fancy, stroked his thick, glossy hair, – which once she had pulled, – smoothed it and twisted it round her fingers? – But he was going away all the same, to far places, where she could not follow him. He did not mind what became of her, but left her here, forlorn, as in her dream. In two or three days he would be gone, he would see the house no more, nor the church, nor the gentle cows in the stable, he would not even hear the Danish language spoken, but some strange tongue, incomprehensible to her, – and she would have gone from his mind – gone, gone, she thought, and bit her hair, that was salt with her tears.

She was now, according to her promise, going to speak to her father, and to get leave for herself and Peter to go to Elsinore. After a while an idea rose to the surface of her mind. How easily could she not make all his great plans void? – If she did tell her father of his project there would be no ships in Peter's life, no rounding of the Horn, no drowning in the water of all the oceans. She sat in her bed crouching on the thought, like a hen on her eggs. Till now, it seemed to her, she managed to keep things at a distance – today they were drawing in upon her, touching her, as she hated things to do, pressing her breast. In the end she got up, and put on her old frock.

Rosa very rarely begged her father for anything. He would give her what she asked, – for the reason, she had been told, that she was so like her mother, after whom she was named. But she did not like to assume, in this way, the part of a dead woman, she wanted to be herself, the young Rosa. So she might some-times apply to him on behalf of Eline or of her child, but for herself she would not do it. Still today she needed the support of both father and mother. Some time ago, to amuse herself, she 71 had put up her hair after the fashion of her mother's hair in her small portrait of her. Now, in front of the little dim mirror she again carefully did it up in the same way. Then she went down to her father's room.

She came out from it again with a blank face, like a doll's, and for some time stood quite still outside it. She had her handkerchief in her hand, with a small pile of money tied up in it, the purchase-price of the cow, which the parson had given her, and told her to hand over to Eline. He had been so deeply moved during their talk together, that he had even covered his face at the idea of his nephew's ingratitude, and again lifted it, marked by tears. As she was about to go, he took her hand and looked at her.

To the parson it was a constant burden and grief that he could not quite believe in the dogma of the resurrection of the body, on which, all the same, he must preach from his pulpit, – for he distrusted and feared the body. The young girl, he thought, would not be tormented by any such doubts. And indeed the flesh that he touched was fresh and clean, one might imagine that it would be admitted to paradise. He had sighed deeply, counted up the money and laid it in her cool, calm hand. To Rosa all ideas of purchase and sale were, for some reason, displeasing, she took it reluctantly, and so unconcernedly, that the old man had reminded her to tie it up in her handkerchief. Now, outside the door, she put the bundle into the pocket of her skirt.

She wanted to strengthen herself in the conviction that she was behaving normally and reasonably, and decided that she would go down to the kitchen, to have her breakfast. On the steps down she heard lively voices in there, and in the kitchen she found the whole household gathered round a fishwife from the coast, who carried fish about for sale in a creel upon her back

These fisherwomen were a brisk, hardy race, they would walk twenty miles, heavy-laden, in all kinds of weather, and come home to cook and darn for a husband and a dozen children They were quick-witted, great newsmongers and at home in every house, and they preferred their roving outdoor profession to that of the peasant-woman, tied up in the stable or by the churn, and to that of the parson's wife. Emma, the fishwife, had placed her creel on the floor and herself upon the chopping-block, she was drinking coffee from a saucer and giving out the news of the neighbourhood, laughing at her own tales. The lump of candy in her mouth, her scarcity of teeth and the broad dialect of her talk, – mixed up with Swedish, for she was a Swede by birth as were many of the fishermen's wives along the Sound, – made it difficult to follow her tales. But the children of the parsonage could speak the dialect themselves, when they wanted to. She broke off her story to nod to the parson's pretty daughter, and Rosa took her own cup of coffee to the chopping-block, to hear the news.

Peter caught sight of the girl, and saw or heard nothing else. After a while he came up and stood close to her, but he did not speak. When the talk and laughter were loud in the kitchen Rosa said, without looking at him: 'I have talked with my father I may go to Elsinore, and you can come with me. Now that the snow is thawing we can go with the waggoners. We may even go today.'

At her news the boy grew pale, as she herself had done when, in the early morning, in bed, she had thought of him. After a long time he said: 'No We cannot go today I shall come up to your room again tonight, there is something more that I have got to tell you.

'I can come, can I not?' he asked.

'Yes,' said Rosa.

Peter went away, to the other end of the kitchen, and came back again. 'The ice is breaking up,' he said, 'Emma has seen it this morning. The Sound is free.'

Emma, for the benefit of the girl, repeated her report. All winter the fishermen had had to walk a long way out on the ice, to catch cod with a tin bait. Now the ice was breaking, the open water was in sight, in a few days they would have their boats afloat once more.

'I shall go down to see it,' said Peter. Rosa glanced at his face, and then could not take her eyes off it again, it was so strangely solemn and radiant, and he knew, she thought, nothing at all of what she knew.

'Come with me, Rosa,' he exclaimed in a great, happy seizure, as if he could not let her out of his sight.

'Yes,' said Rosa.

The little boy, when he heard that they were going to see the ice break up, wanted to come with them. Rosa lifted him up. 'No, you cannot come,' she said to him, 'it is too far away for you, I shall tell you about it, when I come back.'

The child gravely put his hands to her face. 'No, you will never tell me,' he said.

Eline tried to hold back the girl, and told her that it was too far away for her as well.

'Nay, I want to go far away,' said Rosa. She put on an old cloak, and a pair of scabby furred gloves, that belonged to her father, and went out with Peter.

As they came out of the house they saw that the snow was gone from the fields, but that all the same the world was lighter than before, for the air was filled with blurred, resplendent clarity. It almost blinded them, they strove to get up their eyelids against it. On all sides they heard the sound of dripping and running water. The walking was heavy, the melting snow had made the road slippery. Peter set off at a quick pace, and then had to wait impatiently for the girl, who in her old shoes slid and stumbled on the path, she caught him up, warm with the exertion, and giddy, like himself, with the air and the light.

As they walked he stood still. 'Listen,' he said, 'that is the lark.' They kept immovable, close to one another, and did indeed hear, high over their heads, the incessant, triumphant jingle of a lark's shake, a drizzle of ecstasy.

A little further on, in the forest, they came upon a couple of woodcutters, and Peter stopped to talk with them while he chose and cut a long stick for himself and one for Rosa from two young beeches. An old man looked at Rosa, asked if she was the parson's girl at Søllerød, and remarked on how much she had grown. It was rare that the children of the parsonage had talk with outside people. Now, with Emma and the old woodcutter, Rosa felt the world to be opening up to her.

Peter had walked on in a state of blissful intoxication, with the sea before him and dragging him like a magnet, and with the girl so close in his track. After his talk with the woodcutters he had to go on speaking, but could not possibly find words for his own course of thought, so he began to tell her a story.

'I have heard a story, Rosa, you know,' he said, 'of a skipper who named his ship after his wife. He had the figurehead of it beautifully carved, just like her, and the hair of it gilt. But his wife was jealous of the ship. "You think more of the figurehead than of me," she said to him. "No," he answered, "I think so highly of her because she is like you, – yes, because she is you yourself. Is she not gallant, full-bosomed, does she not dance in the waves, like you at our wedding? – In a way she is really even kinder to me than you are, she gallops along where I tell her to go, and she lets her long hair hang down freely, while you put up yours under a cap. But she turns her back to me, so that when I want a kiss I come home to Elsinore."

'Now once, when this skipper was trading to Trankebar, he chanced to help an old native King to flee from traitors in his own country. As they parted the King gave him two big blue, precious stones, and these he had set into the face of his figurehead, like a pair of eyes to it. When he came home he told his wife of his adventure, and said: "Now she has your blue eyes too." "You had better give me the stones for a pair of earrings," said she. "No," he said again, "I cannot do that, and you would not ask me to if you understood." Still the wife could not stop fretting about the blue stones, and one day, when her husband was with the skippers' corporation, she had a glazier of the town take them out, and put two bits of blue glass into the figurehead instead, and the skipper did not find out, but sailed off to Portugal.

'But after some time the skipper's wife found that her eyesight was growing bad, and that she could not see to thread a needle. She went to a wise woman, who gave her ointment and waters, but they did not help her, and in the end the old woman shook her head, and told her that this was a rare and incurable disease, and that she was going blind. "Oh God," the wife then cried, "that the ship was back in the harbour of Elsinore! Then I should have the glass taken out, and the jewels put back. For did he not say that they were my eyes?" But the ship did not come back. Instead the skipper's wife had a letter from the consul of Portugal, who informed her that she had been wrecked, and gone to the bottom with all her hands. And it was a very strange thing, the consul wrote, that in broad daylight she had run straight into a tall rock, rising out of the sea.'

While Peter told his tale they were walking down a hill in the wood, and in the descent Rosa felt something gently knocking against her knee. She put her hand in her pocket, and touched the handkerchief, with the money in it, that she had forgotten to give to Eline. She ran her fingers over it, there ought to be thirty coins there. The figure rang familiar to her mind. Thirty pieces of silver, the purchase-price of a life. She had sold a life, she thought, and had done what Judas Iscariot once did.

The idea had perhaps been in her mind vaguely for some time, ever since she had looked at Peter in the kitchen. As now she put it into words to herself, it hit her with such awful strength that she thought she must fall headlong down the hill. She wavered on her feet, and Peter, in the midst of his story, told her to hold on to him. She heard what he said but she could not answer, and his voice to her seemed to be followed by a dead silence. Although she kept on trudging at the boy's heels she heard neither their footsteps nor the sounds of the wood, but moved on like a deaf person.

So now it had come, she thought, what all her life she had feared and waited for. Here, at last, was the horror which was to kill her.

She did not exactly feel the catastrophe, or the ruin, to have been brought on her by her own fault, she had not got it in her to feel so, but in all calamities would be quick to put the blame on somebody else. But she accepted it in full as her personal lot and portion. It was her fate and her doom, it was the end of her.

The name of Judas stuck in her ear, and kept on ringing there with terrible force. Yes, Judas was her equal, the only human being to whom she could really turn for sympathy or advice, he would show her her way. So strongly did the idea take hold of her that after a minute she looked round, bewildered, for a tree such as Judas had found for himself. They were walking through a glade in the forest, where only a few tall beech-trees grew here and there and, as she gazed about her, a buzzard, the first she had seen that year, loosened itself from a high branch and majestically sailed farther into the wood, with a silver glimmer on its broad, tawny wings. Judas, Rosa reflected, had kissed Christ, when he betrayed him, they must have been such good friends that it came natural to them to kiss one another. She had not kissed Peter, and now they would never kiss, and that was the only difference between her and the accursed apostle.

She did not see the wood round her, or the pale sky above her, she was once more back in her father's room, and at the moment when she had denounced Peter to him. The parson had spoken to her of his youth and had told her how in Copenhagen he had been assistant to the prison chaplain. There he had learnt, he said, that a prison is a good, a safe place for human beings to be in, – he himself still often felt that he might sleep better in a prison than in any other place. Some of the wrong-doers, he told her, had tried to break out, he had pitied their short-sightedness, and had felt it to be to their own good when they were captured and brought back. Then, a moment before with a sigh he took up the money and gave it to her, he had looked her in the face and said: 'But you, Rosa, you do not want to run away, you will stay with me.' Rosa had gazed round the room, then, it had seemed to repeat the same words. It was a poor room, sparsely furnished, with a sanded floor; people laughed, she knew, at the thought that it was a clergyman's study. Yet this room belonged to her, she had known it all her life. Why should anyone, she had thought, disown and desert it any more than she did? Now she had sided with that room, with the prison, with the grave, and had closed the doors of them on her. For she had not guessed it then to be her fate that, if Peter was a prisoner, she herself would no more be free. She remembered the open window of last night, after Peter had gone from her, and the fresh darkness round her pillow. She had closed that window too. She had closed all the windows in the world on her, and never again would she stand in an open window, and let everything come to Peter, on its own, at the sight of her.

Slowly she returned to the world of reality round her, to the wet brown wood, the curves of the road and Peter's figure upon it, bare headed, with a big old muffler round his neck. She did not quite like him, for through him her misery had come, and if he had not been there she would still have walked in the woods, beautiful, content and proud. But it was impossible to her to think of anything upon the earth but him. He stalked on lightly, a strong, straight boy, his head filled with dreams. It was as if she were tied to him with a rope, and were being dragged along after him, a bent, decrepit old woman, so much older than he as to be grieving, as to be weeping over his youth and simplicity.

They again came to the top of a hill, from where there was a view over the lower parts of the wood, blue with the spring mist. Peter stopped, and stood for a minute in silence.

'Do you remember, Rosa,' he said, 'that when we were small we came here to gather wild raspberries? In many years, when we are old people, we shall come back here again. Perhaps then everything will be changed, the wood all cut down, and we shall not know the place. Then we will talk together of today.'

It was, once more, the mystic melancholy of adolescence, which will take in, at the very height of its vitality and with a grave wisdom, that soon again vanishes, both past and future: 79 time itself, in the abstract. Rosa listened to him, but could not understand him. The past she had destroyed, and she shrank from the future with horror. All that she had got in the world, she thought, was this one hour, and their walk to the sea.

In a short time they came to a steep brink, grown with straggly fir-trees, and had the Sound straight before them.

It was a rare and wonderful sight. The ice was breaking up, – a little way out from the coast it still lay solid, a white-grey plane. But already at a short distance from land, clear of the ground and dissipated into floes and sheets, it was gently rocking and swaying, and slowly turning with the current beneath it. And outside the irregular, broken white line was the open sea, pale blue, almost as light as the air, a mighty element, still drowsy after its long winter sleep, but free, wandering on according to its own lustful heart, and embracing all the earth.

There was hardly any wind, but in the air a faint rustle, like a low, joyful chatter, where the sheets of ice rubbed against one another, and thronged to get afloat.

Peter had not touched Rosa since he had played with her hair in bed, now for a second he seized her hand, and in his warm palm she felt a stream of energy and joy. Then in a few long leaps he rushed down the brink and out on the ice, and she ran after him.

If Rosa had been ten or twenty years older she might at this moment have died or gone mad with grief. Now she was so young that her despair itself had vigour in it, and bore her up. Since she had only got this one hour of life left to her, she must, within it, enjoy, experience and suffer to the utmost of her capacity. She bounded on the ice as swift as the boy.

To Rosa the supreme wonder and delight of the scenery lay in the fact that everything was wet. Things had lately been dry and hard, unyielding to the touch, irresponsive to the cry of her heart. But here all flowed and fluctuated, the whole world was fluid. Near the shore there were patches of thin white ice that broke as she trod on them, so that she had to wade through pools of clear water, her shoes soon got soaked, as she ran the water sprinkled over her skirt, and the sense of universal moisture intoxicated her. She felt as if, within a minute or two, she herself, and Peter with her, might melt and dissolve into some unknown, salt flow of delight, and become absorbed into the infinite, swaying, wet world. She seemed to see their two figures quite small upon the white plane. She did not know that her pale face became radiant as she ran on.

Here on the ice Peter waited for her patiently, and kept close to her, more collected and with more weight to him than when on the road he had been swept forward by the wild longing of his soul. They walked or ran side by side. Rosa thought: 'I have gone to sea with Peter, after all.' She made him stop a moment.

'Nay, Peter,' she said, 'look, we are going to Elsinore now. That tall packing of ice out there is Godmother's house. And that one further out, you know, that is the harbour.'

They made straight for her godmother's house; on the way to it Peter said: 'Is it not a strange thing about the sea, Rosa? You may look out over it as over a prairie, all the horizon round. And then, just by turning your eyes, you may look down into it as well, all the way to the bottom of it, and it holds back nothing from you. People sometimes say that the sea is treacherous and the earth trustworthy. But the earth closes itself up to one. There may be anything, just below your feet, – a buried treasure, the treasure of one of the old pirates, – and you can have no idea of it. And as to the air, – you may gaze up into it, but you will never know how it looks from the outside. The sea is a friend.'

They stopped at Rosa's godmother's house, sat down on it, and tried to make out places along the wide, hazy coastline. Two trees formed a landmark above the fishing village of Sletten, they were palm-trees upon a coral island. A glint in the air, from the copper roof of Kronborg Castle, far up north, was the first gleam of the white cliffs of Dover. To the south, a mile away, there were people out on the ice, like themselves, they would be wild men, cannibals, whom they must avoid. 'Yes,' thought Rosa, 'why would he not content himself with such journeys as these? Then we might have been happy.'

As they walked further they had, from time to time, to straddle over deep cracks in the ice, that shone green as glass, the ice was more than two feet thick. Once Rosa imagined that she felt the ground faintly moving under her, and got a strange sensation that something or someone, a third party, had joined in their sea-adventure, but she said nothing to Peter. They kept running and leaping, always side by side. 'Now,' Rosa cried out, 'we are at the harbour of Elsinore.'

The breath of the sea here came straight into their warm, flushed faces. There was a southerly current on the still day, the sheets of ice before them were slowly travelling north.

By the coast of Sealand the wind rarely goes round north from east to west, but it will blow a long time from the east, with rain and foul weather, then change and go south-east and south, to finish up in the west and let the air clear up. Sometimes a calm follows, and, while the wind dozes, the Sound slowly fills with slackened sails from many countries, like loose goosedown, blown together to one side of a pond. Peter and Rosa thought of the ships they had seen gathered here in summer weather.

Now there were tufted ducks swimming in the pale water, themselves so similar to it in colour that they could only be distinguished by their black necks and wings, an irregular, shifting group of little dark specks upon the waves.

'Yes,' Peter said slowly, 'now we are at the harbour of Elsinore. And that,' he added and pointed ahead, 'is the *Esperance*. She is riding at anchor, but she is ready to put to sea.' The *Esperance* was a large floe of ice, fifty feet long, and separated from the ice on which they stood by a long crevice. 'Am I to board her now, Rosa?'

Rosa crossed her arms on her breast. 'Yes, we will go on board now,' she said. 'We shall be in the North Sea before anyone has got the scent of it, and near England. And then some day we will go round the Horn.'

Peter cried: 'Are you coming on board with me?'

'Yes,' said Rosa.

'And sailing with me', he asked, 'all the way, to the South Pole, are you?'

'Yes,' said she.

'Oh Rosa,' said Peter, after a pause.

They strode on to the *Esperance*, and Peter took Rosa's hand and held it. They were both tired with their run on the ice, and pleased to stand still on deck.

Peter looked in front of him, his face lifted. But the girl, after a time, turned her head to see what her native coast of Sealand would look like, from so far out. Then she saw that the crevice between the floe and the land-ice had widened. A clear current of water, six feet wide, ran where they had walked. The *Esperance* had really put to sea. The sight terrified Rosa, she would have shrieked out loud, and run.

She did not shriek, though, she stood immovable, and her hand did not even tremble in Peter's hand. For within the next moment a great calm came upon her. That fate, which all her 83 life she had dreaded, and from which today there was no escape, that, she saw now, was death. It was nothing but death.

For a few minutes she alone was aware of the position. She did not think much, she stood up straight and grave, accepting her destiny. Yes, they were to die here, she and Peter, to drown. Peter now would never know that she had betrayed him. It did not matter any longer either, she might quite well tell him herself. She was once more Rosa, the gift to the world, and to Peter too. At the moment when she collected her whole being to meet death, Rosa did not grieve for herself. But she mourned, sadly, for the sake of the world, which was to lose Rosa. So much loveliness, so much inspiration, so many sweet benefactions, were to go from it, now.

Peter felt the slight swaying of the ice-sheet, spun round, and saw that they were adrift. His heart gave two or three tremendous throbs, he shifted his grip from the girl's arm to her elbow, and swung her with him to the edge of the floe. He saw, then, that he might possibly jump the channel, but that Rosa could not do it. So he again dragged her back a little, and looked round. There was clear water on all sides. The people whom they had seen on the ice were no longer in sight. The two were alone with the sea and the sky.

Bewildered and trembling the boy tore at his hair with one hand, still holding her elbow with the other. 'And I myself begged you to come with me!' he cried out.

After a moment he turned round towards her, and this was the first time since they had come out of the house that he looked at her. Her round face was quiet, she gazed at him beneath the long eyelashes, as from an ambush.

'Now we are sailing straight to Elsinore,' she said, 'it is better than that we should go home first, do you not see?'

Peter stared at her, and slowly the blood went up in his face, till it was all aflame. Their danger, and his own guilt in bringing her here, vanished and came to nothing before the fact that a girl could be so glorious. As he kept looking at her, all his life, and his dreams of the future, passed before him. He remembered, too, that he was to have come up to her room that night, and at the thought a swift, keen pain ran through him. Yet this was more wonderful than anything else.

'When we come to Elsinore,' Rosa said, 'where the Sound is narrow, the captain of the *Esperance* himself will see us, and fetch us on to his ship, do you not think?'

The boy's heart was filled to the brim with adoration, he felt the light wind in his hair and the smell of the sea in his nostrils, and the movement of the water, which terrified Rosa, intoxicated him; it was impossible that he should not hope, it could not be that he should not have faith in his star. It seemed to him, at this moment, that for a long time, perhaps for the length of his whole life, he had been lifted from one ecstasy into another, and that this might well be the crowning miracle of it all. He had never been afraid to die, but he could not, now, give room to the idea of death, for he had not before felt life to be so mighty. At the same time, just as dream and reality seemed, on the floe, to have become one, so did the distinction between life and death seem to have been done away with. Dimly he reflected that this state of things would be what was meant by the word immortality. So he looked no more ahead or behind, the hour held him.

He let go his grip on Rosa's arm, and again looked round. He went to pick up their walking-sticks, that they had flung away as they came on to the *Esperance.* He was some time boring a hole in the ice with his knife, so as to make fast his stick in it, and in tying his big old red handkerchief to the top of the stick, now it would serve them as a flag of distress, and be seen from far off. He tied the knife to Rosa's stick with a bit of cord from his pocket, to turn it into a boathook – if ever the current should bear them close to the land-ice he might get a grip on it with the hook. Rosa looked on.

With the raising of the flag their floe became a different thing from the others round them, a ship, a home on the water for him and her. It was not cold! A silver light had come into the sky. A curious idea ran through Peter's head, he wished that he had brought his flute, to play to her as they sailed, for till now she had never cared to hear him.

In his pocket he had a bottle with gin in it, he fished it up, and asked Rosa to drink from it. It would do her good, he said, and he would himself have some after her. Rosa strongly disliked the smell of gin, and had before been angry with Peter for drinking it, now, after hesitating a little, she consented to taste it, and even to drink out of the bottle, for they had no glass. The few drops that she swallowed at first made her cough, and brought tears into her eyes, but for Peter's sake she had a second draught, which warmed her all through, and Peter had a pull at the bottle himself and set it down on the ice. When again she recovered her breath she said: 'Gin is not really a bad thing, after all.'

Peter pulled off his coat and muffler, and wrapped them round Rosa, crossing the muffler over her breast, and she let him do so without a word.

'Why have you put up your hair today?' he asked her.

Rosa only shook her head in reply, it would be too long to explain.

'Let it hang down,' he said, 'then the wind will blow in it.'

'Nay, I cannot get my arms up, with your muffler on,' said Rosa.

'Can I take it down?' he asked.

'Yes,' said she.

Peter with skilled fingers, trained at the rigging of the barque *Rosa*, undid the ribbon that held up her hair, as she stood patiently, with her head a little bent, close to him. The soft, glossy mass of hair loosened and tumbled down, covering her cheeks, neck and bosom, and just as he had foretold, the wind lifted the tresses, and gently swept them against his face.

At that moment suddenly, without any warning, the ice broke beneath their feet, as if they had stepped on a hidden crack in it, and their combined weight had made it give way. The break threw them on to their knees, and to one another. For a minute the ice still bore them, a foot below the surface of the water. They might have saved themselves then, if they had separated and struggled on to the two sides of the crack, but the idea did not occur to either of them.

Peter, as he felt himself flung off his balance, and the ice-cold water round his feet, in one great movement clasped his arms round Rosa and held her to him. And at this last moment the fantastic, unknown feeling of having no ground under him in his consciousness was mingled with the unknown sense of softness, of her body against his. Rosa squeezed her face into his collarbone, and shut her eyes.

The current was strong; they were swept down, in one another's arms, in a few seconds.

MARTIN AMIS · *God's Dice*

HANS CHRISTIAN ANDERSEN *The Emperor's New Clothes*

MARCUS AURELIUS *Meditations*

JAMES BALDWIN *Sonny's Blues*

AMBROSE BIERCE *An Occurrence at Owl Creek Bridge*

DIRK BOGARDE *From Le Pigeonnier*

WILLIAM BOYD *Killing Lizards*

POPPY Z BRITE · *His Mouth will Taste of Wormwood*

ITALO CALVINO *Ten Italian Folktales*

ALBERT CAMUS *Summer*

TRUMAN CAPOTE *First and Last*

RAYMOND CHANDLER · *Goldfish*

ANTON CHEKHOV *The Black Monk*

ROALD DAHL *Lamb to the Slaughter*

ELIZABETH DAVID *I'll be with You in the Squeezing of a Lemon*

N. J. DAWOOD (TRANS.) *The Seven Voyages of Sindbad the Sailor*

ISAK DINESEN *The Dreaming Child*

SIR ARTHUR CONAN DOYLE *The Man with the Twisted Lip*

DICK FRANCIS · *Racing Classics*

SIGMUND FREUD · *Five Lectures on Psycho-Analysis*

KAHLIL GIBRAN *Prophet, Madman, Wanderer*

STEPHEN JAY GOULD *Adam's Navel*

ALASDAIR GRAY *Five Letters from an Eastern Empire*

GRAHAM GREENE *Under the Garden*

JAMES HERRIOT *Seven Yorkshire Tales*

PATRICIA HIGHSMITH *Little Tales of Misogyny*

M. R JAMES AND R L STEVENSON *The Haunted Dolls' House*

RUDYARD KIPLING *Baa Baa, Black Sheep*

PENELOPE LIVELY *A Long Night at Abu Simbel*

KATHERINE MANSFIELD · *The Escape*

READ MORE IN PENGUIN

For complete information about books available from Penguin and how to order them, please write to us at the appropriate address below. Please note that for copyright reasons the selection of books varies from country to country.

IN THE UNITED KINGDOM: Please write to *Dept. JC, Penguin Books Ltd, FREEPOST, West Drayton, Middlesex UB7 0BR.*

If you have any difficulty in obtaining a title, please send your order with the correct money, plus ten per cent for postage and packaging, to *PO Box No. 11, West Drayton, Middlesex UB7 0BR.*

IN THE UNITED STATES: Please write to *Consumer Sales, Penguin USA, P.O. Box 999, Dept. 17109, Bergenfield, New Jersey 07621-0120.* VISA and MasterCard holders call 1-800-253-6476 to order all Penguin titles.

IN CANADA: Please write to *Penguin Books Canada Ltd, 10 Alcorn Avenue, Suite 300, Toronto, Ontario M4V 3B2.*

IN AUSTRALIA: Please write to *Penguin Books Australia Ltd, P.O. Box 257, Ringwood, Victoria 3134.*

IN NEW ZEALAND: Please write to *Penguin Books (NZ) Ltd, Private Bag 102902, North Shore Mail Centre, Auckland 10.*

IN INDIA: Please write to *Penguin Books India Pvt Ltd, 706 Eros Apartments, 56 Nehru Place, New Delhi 110 019.*

IN THE NETHERLANDS: Please write to *Penguin Books Netherlands bv, Postbus 3507, NL-1001 AH Amsterdam.*

IN GERMANY: Please write to *Penguin Books Deutschland GmbH, Metzlerstrasse 26, 60594 Frankfurt am Main.*

IN SPAIN: Please write to *Penguin Books S. A., Bravo Murillo 19, 10 B, 28015 Madrid.*

IN ITALY: Please write to *Penguin Italia s.r.l., Via Felice Casati 20, I-20124 Milano.*

IN FRANCE: Please write to *Penguin France S. A., 17 rue Lejeune, F-31000 Toulouse.*

IN JAPAN: Please write to *Penguin Books Japan, Ishikiribashi Building, 2-5-4, Suido, Bunkyo-ku, Tokyo 112.*

IN GREECE: Please write to *Penguin Hellas Ltd, Dimocritou 3, GR-106 71 Athens.*

IN SOUTH AFRICA: Please write to *Longman Penguin Southern Africa (Pty) Ltd, Private Bag X08, Bertsham 2013.*